MW00387849

CAFFEINE CAN KILL

Lydia,
It was nice meeting
you. Enjoy the book!

Bob Doerr

Bob Doerr

TTP

TotalRecall Publications, Inc.
1103 Middlecreek
Friendswood, Texas 77546
281-992-3131   281-482-5390 Fax
www.totalrecallpress.com

All rights reserved. Except as permitted under the United States Copyright Act of 1976, No part of this publication may be reproduced, stored in a retrieval system, or transmitted in any form or by any means electronic or mechanical or by photocopying, recording, or otherwise without prior permission of the publisher. Exclusive worldwide content publication / distribution by TotalRecall Publications, Inc.

Copyright © 2015 by: Bob Doerr
All rights reserved
ISBN: 978-1-59095-562-8
UPC: 6-43977-45625-0

Library of Congress Control Number: 2015932509

Printed in the United States of America with simultaneous printings in Australia, Canada, and United Kingdom.

FIRST EDITION
1 2 3 4 5 6 7 8 9 10

This is a work of fiction. The characters, names, events, views, and subject matter of this book are either the author's imagination or are used fictitiously. Any similarity or resemblance to any real people, real situations or actual events is purely coincidental and not intended to portray any person, place, or event in a false, disparaging or negative light.

The scanning, uploading and distribution of this book via the Internet or via any other means without the permission of the publisher is illegal and punishable by law. Please purchase only authorized electronic editions, and do not participate in or encourage electronic piracy of copyrighted materials. Your support of the author's rights is appreciated.

To my father who inspired me to
pursue the craft of writing.

About the Author

Award winning author Bob Doerr grew up in a military family, graduated from the Air Force Academy, and had a career of his own in the Air Force. In the Air Force, Bob specialized in criminal investigations and counterintelligence gaining significant insight to the worlds of crime, espionage and terrorism. His work brought him into close coordination with the CIA, FBI, and the security agencies of many different countries. His education credits include a Masters in International Relations from Creighton University. A full time author, this is his seventh mystery/thriller. His books have won numerous awards. His most recent Jim West mystery, **No One Else to Kill,** was a winner in the 2013 Eric Hoffer Awards. The Military Writers Society of America selected Bob Doerr as their Author of the Year for 2013. Bob lives in Garden Ridge, Texas, with Leigh, his wife of 41 years.

About the Book

This Jim West mystery/thriller, the sixth in the series, finds Jim traveling to the Texas Hill Country to attend the grand opening of a friend's winery and vineyard. Upon arriving in Fredericksburg, Jim witnesses a brutal kidnapping at a local coffee shop. The next morning while driving down an unpaved country road to the grand opening, he comes across an active crime scene barely a quarter mile from his friend's winery. A Fredericksburg policeman who talked to Jim the day before at the kidnapping scene recognizes Jim and asks him to identify the body of a dead young woman as the woman who was kidnapped. Jim does, and as a result of this unwelcome relationship with the police is asked the next morning to identify the body of another murdered person as the man who had kidnapped the young woman. A third murder throws Jim's vacation into complete disarray and draws Jim and a female friend into the sights of one of the killers.

Chapter 1

The smell of the fresh brewing coffee hit me as I entered the Starbucks clone and joined the two people ahead of me in line. I thought the girl right in front of me should still be in school, high school, rather than here at the coffee shop, until I saw the wedding ring on her finger. She looked sixteen and too thin. Her straight blond hair had a few streaks of pink above each ear.

The guy in front of her had already paid, but instead of moving away from the register, he stood there complaining about the Cowboys' loss to the Bears the night before. The girl edged in closer to the register. I imagined she was trying to catch the eye of the cashier. I didn't blame her for being impatient, because the guy was cutting into our time.

"Excuse me," she said softly.

Good for her, I thought. That's when I noticed the anxious look on her face. I know a lot of us need our caffeine fix each day, but something more than the cup of coffee had to be troubling her. She looked afraid.

She ordered a fancy drink that took at least four words to identify and paid by credit card. She went over to the waiting area to stand by the Cowboys fan and another woman who picked at the sleeve of her dark blouse. They all stared at the counter, trained like we all are to wait for our drinks to appear.

Knowing that the cost of a beverage goes up with every additional word, I kept my order to two words and handed the cashier my credit card. I hated charging such a small amount on my card, but I'd been meaning to hit an ATM ever since I left home and hadn't yet.

"Thanks, Jim. Would you like a receipt?" the cashier asked. She wore a hat with a number of medals fastened to the brim. She didn't really know who I was. I hadn't been to this coffee shop before. She had gotten my name from my credit card.

"No--"

A scream interrupted my response, and all hell broke loose.

I turned and saw a man wearing a New York Giants hoodie enter the café waving a large revolver in his right hand. His left hand pointed a finger at the girl who had stood in line in front of me, but his eyes roamed the room looking for someone.

"Where is he?" the gunman spat the words out. He looked at me, and I instinctively raised both hands in front of me to show him I was no threat. His eyes didn't look right. I figured this guy was either off some very important meds or had overdosed on something.

"There is no one. I told you before-"

"Liar!" he shouted at the young girl. He took two steps and smacked the girl across the face with the barrel of the revolver.

She collapsed to the floor clutching her face. She remained conscious, but I could tell the blow had stunned her.

"Hey," a coffee shop employee yelled at the guy with the gun. He had been wiping off a nearby table. "Leave her alone."

A brave guy, I thought. He had black hair and a closely shaved beard across his chin. What he did next, however, wasn't very smart. He took a step toward the guy with the gun.

Bam!! The man fired once, and the bullet hit the coffee shop guy in the belly. They both stood there for a second staring at each other. The guy with the bullet in his gut fell straight down into a sitting position. He stared at his belly, and a strange sound started emanating from his mouth.

"Anyone else?" the crazy guy shouted to the rest of us as he waved his gun back and forth.

I thought he might actually shoot someone else. He didn't. He reached down and grabbed the girl by her hair and yanked her up. He started backing out the door before she had her balance. She staggered backwards and screamed a few choice words at him. He didn't pay any attention to her. He held on to her and pulled her with him to an old gray van. He never let go of her as he opened a side panel door and shoved her in. He closed the door behind her, jumped into the driver's seat, and sped away.

I hurried outside, furious at myself for not being able to do more to protect the girl. I took a picture of the back of the van with my smart phone, hoping to get the license tag. I dialed 911. When I looked back inside, it looked like everyone had grabbed their phones. I imagined everyone else was also calling 911.

"I want to report a shooting and a kidnapping," I said to the 911 operator. I told her where, and she said someone had already called it in.

"I'm going to try to follow the van the guy left in," I said and was about to hang up when she instructed me in no uncertain words not to leave the scene.

"But I-"

"The police will be there any second. Do not leave," she said again.

"Ok."

I went back into the café. Everyone stood in a big circle

around the wounded employee. Another barista knelt down next to him and pressed a white towel against his wound. She looked older than the other employees, and I wondered if she was the manager. Two of the younger female employees hugged each other crying. I heard someone whisper, "Is he going to die?"

Two customers who had been sitting at a corner table hurried outside to their cars. They had to pass me on their way out. "You aren't supposed to leave," I said. My voice came out without much emphasis. They ignored me.

"Hey, the cops said no one is supposed to leave the scene," one of the male baristas went to the door and shouted after them. They ignored him and drove off. He walked over to the wounded guy and knelt over. "Hang in there, Cisco. I can hear the ambulance coming. You're going to be okay."

Cisco didn't reply. He kept staring at his stomach.

An ambulance rolled to a stop in the parking lot. Two guys rushed out and took charge of their patient. Three or four of the people in the small crowd around the victim started telling the medics what happened.

"Thank you, thank you, but please tell the story to the police. We need to focus all our attention on this man," one of the medical technicians said.

A woman in an oversized red flannel shirt, one of the people who had tried to tell the medics what happened, looked upset that they had cut her off in the middle of her story. She mumbled something that I didn't catch, but two people close to her glanced at her with a disapproving look.

"Everyone please back away and give us some room," one of the medics said.

A few people started to move away, but the majority appeared unwilling to give up their ringside seats.

"Hey let's all back away and give them some space," I said in a loud voice. No one even looked in my direction.

"He's right. Back away, please. If you gather over there in that part of the room, we'll be passing out a free refill." The man who spoke was the same man who called after the two customers who had fled the scene. I noticed his name tag identified him as the manager. He had short reddish brown hair and looked like he hadn't shaved in a few days. I placed him in his late twenties or early thirties. He said something to the staff, and they all returned to their work stations.

The offer of a free refill did the trick. All but the woman in the red flannel shirt moved away from the wounded man. I could tell the woman still wanted to tell her story, but the two men working to save the wounded employee had no interest in her.

A Fredericksburg police car drove into the parking lot. Two men in uniform climbed out of the car and hurried into the coffee shop. The woman in the red flannel shirt went straight to them. One of the policemen stopped to listen to her. The other continued to the two medical technicians and the victim. The policeman talked briefly to the medics and the victim. One of the med techs left the huddle and hurried out to the ambulance. A moment later, the policeman approached the counter and asked for the manager.

"Here's another cappuccino for you, Jim." The cute barista who had taken my order handed me another cup.

"Good memory," I said.

"The computer," she said as an explanation. She looked a

lot paler than she had earlier.

"Are you going to be okay?"

"Yes, but poor Cisco; is he going to die?"

"He should make it," I said. I figured he would, but what else could I tell her anyway. "You might want to tell her that she should wash the blood off her arm."

"Oooh!" she hurried over to the employee who had held the white towel against Cisco's bullet wound until the ambulance arrived. She had a drink in both hands and approached the group of customers. About half way between her wrist and her elbow there was a patch of drying blood. It looked like she had washed her hands but hadn't notice the blood on the back of her arm.

Cisco waved feebly at the crowd when they finally rolled him out of the café. A few people shouted encouraging comments to him, but most were preoccupied with the police or their own thoughts.

I spent nearly two hours at the coffee shop mostly waiting to be interviewed before answering questions that I knew would be little help to the investigation. Other than stating what I witnessed, which was the same thing everyone else saw, I couldn't provide any additional insight. The young cop who interviewed me asked if I noticed anything special about the shooter. I had to admit I didn't. I gave him rough height, weight, and physical description. I told him about the handgun.

He wanted to know if I noticed any tattoos or scars. The guy had on jeans and a hoodie sweatshirt, so I had to admit that I hadn't. He brought me back to the guy's hands and asked me if I noticed any tattoos. I told him my eyes focused on the revolver, nothing else. The cop told me to wait around, that they would release us all before long.

My frustration turned to anger targeted primarily at myself. I wanted to kick myself for not jumping into my Mustang and following the van before calling 911. I should have known that the 911 operator would have standard operating procedures that would include telling civilians to not chase after dangerous, armed criminals. If I had delayed my call until after I had started my chase, I could've at least stayed with the van until a police car replaced me in the pursuit. Plus, I knew I could've blown off the instructions and taken up the chase, but I hadn't. At the moment, my acquiescence didn't sit well with me.

At one point, I counted ten different cops there at the scene. Two of the ten were women, but I didn't pay much attention to any of them. The one who appeared to be in charge was my age, mid to late forties, with a puffy, reddish face that made me want to tell him to go see a doctor. I heard one of the other policemen refer to him as Lieutenant. He reassured everyone that they, the police, would have the bad guy soon. A security camera had captured the description and tag number of the van. I offered the police the picture I took. One of the policemen looked at it and sent it on to a number at their headquarters.

"We've got a dragnet set up around the city. He'll never get out of town," the Lieutenant told us. I hadn't heard the term dragnet used in a long time. I hoped he was right.

"Who were they?" one of the customers asked.

"We have her name, and we're working on his. We'll have it soon."

"Are they from here?" the same customer asked.

"Not from Fredericksburg, but we think she's from the Hill Country. Listen, I really can't say anything more at this time."

I heard a few customers or employees try to follow up with a question, but the Lieutenant ignored them and started talking to a couple of the cops who were near him.

The Hill Country of Texas is vast. Over twenty counties claim to be in its several thousands of square miles. Its beauty has made it a popular place for settlers of old and retirees in today's world. The cop said she was from the Hill Country, like saying she's from around here. Typical Texan attitude, I thought. The whole state of New Jersey could hide in the Hill Country.

Chapter 2

I had a hard time sleeping that night. It wasn't the hotel, the bed, or the traffic outside. I just couldn't keep my mind off the young woman. Why didn't I do something? I kept tossing, turning, and telling myself there wasn't anything I could have done. However, the guilt wouldn't go away. I kept trying to come up with possible reasons the man had come looking for her. For some reason, I couldn't imagine that she had married that guy.

At six, I got up and went down to breakfast. The La Quinta hotel chain offers a breakfast that makes life easy for me when I'm on the road. I don't need much when I get up in the morning, but if I don't have at least a cup of coffee and a piece of toast, I'd be out looking for a restaurant. Not that going to a restaurant is a bad thing. It's just not as convenient as having breakfast served where you are.

The television in the breakfast room displayed CNN and the national news. A nasty cold front had the Northeast in its grip, and the CNN crowd thought those of us in the Southwest really cared about that. Of course, even I enjoyed seeing those cars slide uncontrollably down an icy road, as long as no one gets hurt.

I had driven down from Clovis, New Mexico, because a friend of mine invited me to the grand opening of his vineyard and wine making operation. It had been a rough year for me, and this sounded like fun. I came to Fredericksburg a day early to scope out the available real estate in the area. I didn't think I had any real intention of moving away from Clovis, but moving down here had been an idea that wouldn't go away.

The shooting at the coffee shop messed up my appointment with the local realtor. He had scheduled three hours with me yesterday morning. Unfortunately, he had another appointment with someone else in the afternoon. I spent the afternoon by myself driving around. I checked out two new developments and a ranch house for sale by owner. My mind wasn't in it. I spent more time looking around for the van that the guy drove off in with the girl than actually evaluating the real estate.

The local news on the night before admitted, despite what the cop had said, that they had not been able to find the girl, the guy, or the van. The search had been extended into the surrounding counties. The state police and even the FBI had joined the effort. Kidnapping, the announcer reminded us, is a federal offense. The report ended with one piece of good news: the wounded employee was in stable condition.

This morning, the CNN reporters didn't appear to have any interest in what had happened in Fredericksburg, Texas, so I went and asked the receptionist if the television channel could be changed to a local news station. He must have been asked that before, because it didn't take him a second to tell me that there were no local television news shows in the morning.

I made a waffle and drank some more coffee before heading back to my room. I didn't need to be at the Broken Spur Vineyards until noon, and the drive would only take twenty minutes. I decided to kill the morning by walking to the Nimitz museum and spending some time there. I'd been there before, but it had been a long time. The October morning was pleasant, and the long walk made me feel better. However, it didn't take my mind off the incident the day before.

What people in the area still refer to as the Nimitz Museum had grown since the last time I passed through Fredericksburg. Admiral Nimitz ran the war in the Pacific during most of World War II. He also happened to be a local boy. The name of the place had been officially changed to the National Museum of the Pacific War. Despite the name change, I still found the museum fascinating.

I don't know if it was my natural inclination to admire the men and women who sacrificed so much for the country or my appreciation for the magnitude of that war, but I found myself nowhere near done with my self-guided tour when I had to leave. At some future date, I'd have to come back here and spend a whole day in the museum.

The drive to the Broken Spur Vineyards took me about twenty miles east of Fredericksburg, toward Austin. I never knew that Texas had a wine region. To my surprise, this stretch of Highway 290 seemed almost crowded with vineyards. It would take a week to visit them all. I could see why Tom might want to start his business here, but he definitely had a lot of competition.

I had known Tom Hasben for a long time. We had been assigned together at two different air force bases. At Offutt AFB in Omaha, we'd been neighbors, and later in Washington D.C. our paths crossed again. He was a big sports fan, and we attended a few big league games together in Washington. I had also played golf with him a lot. He wasn't very good at golf, so we were a good match.

The invite to the grand opening had surprised me. First, I

thought he still lived in the D.C. area, and second, we hadn't communicated at all since my retirement from the military. The lack of contact wasn't caused by anything negative. I simply never have had the urge to stay in contact with people. I'd like to think most guys are like that, and that I didn't have some character flaw – not that I really worried about it.

I started looking for the turnoff. My invitation explained that the road didn't have a name to it yet, but that I would find it about a mile or so past the Highway 1376 intersection. A temporary sign announcing the grand opening would identify it. I saw the sign in plenty of time and turned off 290. That's when I noticed all the police lights.

No more than a hundred yards from the main road stood a patch of trees with some thick underbrush. A number of police vehicles were parked on and off the road near the trees. I saw an ambulance with its flashers still on. A young sheriff's deputy blocked the narrow road I drove on.

"What's going on?" I asked the officer as he walked up to my window.

"Police business." He studied my Mustang for a minute. "What brings you out here?"

"I'm heading to the Broken Spur Vineyards."

"The grand opening?" he asked.

"Yes."

"Doubt if it will happen today, but you can drive around. Stay left of the road and the cars."

I began my slow drive around the vehicles, and my car bounced over the bumpy, hard ground. At least it was dry. I started to pull back onto the road once I passed the last of the police cars, when I heard someone shouting nearby.

"Hold on!" a voice bellowed from my right.

I stopped the car and looked around. The policeman in charge of the crime scene the day before at the coffee shop waved both hands at me to stop. It didn't take me a second to realize this wasn't any good. He wouldn't have any jurisdiction out here. Whatever or whoever caused all the other law enforcement personnel to show up out here resulted in his being here, too. I climbed out of the Mustang as he approached.

"What's up, Lieutenant?" I asked.

"You were there yesterday, right?" he asked.

I could've asked where. I could've asked why, but I didn't. "Yes, I was there."

"Thought I recognized you," he said. "What's your name again?"

"Jim West."

"Oh yeah, I remember. What are you doing out here?"

"Going to the grand opening at the Broken Spur."

He nodded and looked at me for a few seconds. "Come over here for a second."

"Lieutenant Martin, what's up?" I asked, although I thought I knew.

He either didn't catch or chose to ignore the frustration in my voice.

"I'll tell you in a second. Come on," he said and motioned with his head for me to follow him. He walked toward the gaggle of cops.

I followed him, and we approached two men standing between two county sheriff sedans. "Sheriff, this here is Jim West. He was at the coffee shop yesterday and might be able to confirm the victim's identity."

"Did you call him to come out here?" the sheriff asked.

"No," Martin answered.

I could sense a little tension between the two.

"He's headed to the Broken Spur. Today was supposed to be its grand opening. I saw him and stopped him. We were just saying that we needed someone to corroborate what we had."

"Yeah, okay," the sheriff said with no hint of an apology in his voice. "Jerry, take him to identify the body."

I started to tell them both that I never agreed to look at the dead body and to find someone else, but Jerry preempted me by offering his hand.

"Jerry Stephens," he said. "Would you mind?"

"I'd rather be drinking wine, but okay."

"Those two aren't the best of friends, but they're both okay guys. Have you ever seen a dead body before, Mr. West?" he asked while he walked me toward an overgrown area beneath the trees. The police had placed a tarp between some trees to keep anyone passing by from seeing the scene.

"Unfortunately, yes." I knew it. That's what would have gotten Lieutenant Martin out here.

"This won't be pleasant, but we appreciate your help." He paused for a second in case I had anything to say. I didn't. "Did you get a good look at the girl who was kidnapped?"

"Damn," I said to myself.

"What?"

"Oh, nothing, let's get this over with."

"Excuse me, guys," Deputy Stephens said to the crime scene investigators. "This gentleman needs to view the victim."

Her open eyes stared straight up at the sky. After the eyes, the first thing I noticed was the patch of pink hair above the ear and the red blood stains in her otherwise blond hair. I looked at her face and turned away. I didn't want to remember her like this.

"Is that her? The girl abducted from the coffee shop yesterday?" Stephens asked.

"Yes."

"Are you going to be okay?" he asked me.

"Yeah."

"Did you know anything about her?"

"No. I only saw her that once."

"Come on. Let's move away from here and let them do their work. I know that was gruesome. Sorry you had to see it."

The gruesome sight did bother me. It would bother anyone. Her throat had been slit, and her mouth looked like it had been violently struck before she died. But the scene did not cause me to turn away. I had been around enough death to handle seeing a dead body. The victim herself affected me. The young woman who had stood so close to me the day before and had been snatched right under my nose now lay there dead. I felt terrible for her, and despite knowing better, I took her death personally.

"Can I see your driver's license, Jim? I need to annotate a few things."

"Sure." I gave it to him, and he wrote what he needed down on a form.

He handed it back to me. "From New Mexico," he said, and I nodded. "It says Jim on your license. Is that for James?"

"No, just what it says. Always been a Jim, never been a James," I said.

"Oh," he said it like he wasn't sure if I knew my own name.

"Where are you staying while you're here?"

"The La Quinta, in Fredericksburg."

"You going to be here a few days?"

"Yes. The Lieutenant has my contact data, too," I said.

"Okay."

"Do you know how long she's been out here?" I asked.

"I'm not sure," he said. "We'll know soon."

I didn't know if he knew and didn't think it was any of my business, or if he really didn't know. This wasn't television where everything had to be solved in forty minutes.

They let me go, and I drove the rest of the way to the vineyard. I didn't see as many cars parked in front of the Hasbens' house as I expected. A small group of individuals stood on a large, wooden side deck. They all stared in my direction as I climbed out of the Mustang. The house looked new, like it had been built in the last year or two. I couldn't help but wonder how much money they had sunk into this venture. I could see rows of grapevines extending for some distance behind the house.

"Jim! Jim, is that you?" Tom shouted from the deck.

"No one else," I said.

Tom came off the deck, and we met half way. We shook hands and he grabbed my arm. "Come on, I want you to meet a few friends." He half pulled me toward the deck.

"How've you been doing?" I asked.

"Great," he said. His voice sounded a little forced. "So glad you could make it."

"Jim," a woman called through an open side window. The door to the deck opened and Tom's wife, Brenda, hurried out and gave me a hug. "You haven't changed a bit," she said.

"Me? I've gotten fatter and greyer, but you still look great, Brenda." She did, too. She stood a shade over five feet tall, with dark hair that gave no hint of ever going grey. I thought she was still too pretty for Tom.

"Did you see the police cars?" she whispered to me.

"Yes. I hope it won't put a damper on your opening."

"It already has," she said. I could sense disappointment and even a little anger in her voice.

"Now, Brenda, there's nothing we can do about it," Tom said. "Jim, I want you to meet our guests."

The guests included five couples and three singles. Under the best of circumstances, I would've had a hard time remembering all the names, and today my mind wasn't at its best. However, over the next three hours I got most of them sorted out. Only one more couple arrived after me. I could see the disappointment in Tom's and Brenda's faces. A young guy in his early thirties who was there by himself left shortly after my arrival. He worked for Tom on occasion and had stopped by that morning to help the Hasbens prepare for the event.

"Hard to believe we had fifty people RSVP that they would be coming," Brenda said to me when it became evident they wouldn't even hit twenty. We were in the kitchen alone at the time.

"Not your fault. I can imagine most people turned around when they saw what was going on with the police," I said.

"Do you think we were insensitive? We could've cancelled it and held something later."

"Don't second guess your decision. It's a terrible thing that happened, but it has nothing to do with you other than the fact that the body was left on your property."

"That's not even our property, Jim. The front of our property starts between here and there. We spent so much money for the catering and time on the prep work. The success of this winery is critical to us. Oh, I don't know, maybe we should've cancelled the whole thing."

"When did you hear about police being out there?" I had already looked and realized they couldn't see the police cars from the house. A handful of large oaks and smaller cedars blocked the view.

"Tom went out this morning to put up the sign and saw the van. He stopped to check it out on his way back from the highway. He said it looked abandoned."

I didn't remember seeing the van, but it could've been there among the rest of the vehicles. I had focused on the body, even before I saw it.

"Did he see her?" I asked.

"Yes. He said the van was empty, but when he looked around, he saw something that caught his eye, a patch of clothing."

"I'm surprised he didn't say something to me about finding her," I said. Although he had spent a career in the Air Force, I knew Tom wasn't exactly the steely-eyed-killer type. He definitely had his sensitive side, and finding the dead girl would have been hard on him.

"He said he wasn't going to talk about it today and didn't want anyone else to. This was supposed to be a day of celebration."

"Sorry I brought it up."

"You didn't. I did," she said and grabbed the platter of deviled eggs she had refilled. "Let's join the fun." She seemed to force a smile, and we walked back out to the others.

Tom's desire to keep the conversation away from the dead girl lasted longer than I thought it would. We ate our way through a lot of appetizers and had a lengthy row of empty wine bottles lining the edge of the deck. I guess most of us felt obligated to eat more than we might normally, since so few had shown up.

"Think they're still out there?" Samuel, "everyone calls me Bull," Durham asked the group. Bull owned a nearby ranch and, although it hadn't been explained to me, had some involvement in Tom's purchase of the land.

"You mean the sheriff?" Bull's wife Torry asked.

"Yeah," he answered.

"Probably gone by now," Theo said. Theo owned a car dealership in Fredericksburg and evidently knew more than anyone else in the whole world about wine. I got the impression his unsolicited lectures about this grape or that wine bored more of the guests than just me.

"It's been awfully hot lately. Think we'll get any rain this week?" Tom asked in an obvious attempt to change the topic.

"Could," Lynn said. She had come with her husband, who seemed the quiet sort. Lynn, a licensed real estate broker, helped Tom and Brenda do the actual purchase and had stayed close, especially with Brenda. Unlike her husband, Lynn talked a lot. She also wore a tight, red blouse that I found hard not to look at. "If this was a TV show they'd be long gone and would've already solved the case."

I could see Tom didn't like that his attempt at changing the topic had flopped. "Now, let's not--"

"Tom, who did they find out there? You must know," the

thin guy with short cut red hair interrupted Tom. I couldn't think of his name, but I remembered that he was a neighbor and had a cattle ranch. Tom had referred to the ranch as being big, really big.

"Yeah, Tom, who was it?" Lynn asked.

If Brenda had told anyone else about Tom's desire to not discuss the topic, she wasn't getting much support.

"I don't know. Some poor young woman named Wilkins or Walikins. I'd never seen her before."

"My God, Tom, did you see the body?" Sylvia Scott asked. She was a woman who came to the opening by herself. Brenda had told me that Sylvia managed a small wine distribution operation based in Fredericksburg.

"Unfortunately," Tom said.

"Could the name have been Wilikin? Frances Wilikin?" Theo asked. All of a sudden, he looked shaken.

"You mean that cute girl who wanted a job?" his wife Angie asked.

I didn't understand the relevance, but the name or possible connection to Theo got everyone's attention. I saw Theo nod to his wife.

"Could've been," Tom said, "but like I said, I don't really know."

"How was she killed?" Sylvia asked.

"God, Sylvia, I don't want to think about it," Tom said. "Let me get us some more wine." He went back inside the house.

Brenda followed him in.

"I don't know her name either," I said. Although no one asked for my participation in the conversation, I hoped I might be able to answer everyone's questions and get us off the topic by the time Tom came back out. "However, she was the same young lady who was kidnapped from the coffee shop yesterday. I imagine most of you heard about that."

The majority of the guests nodded in the affirmative or said yes.

"She had been beaten and her throat had been cut. I don't know if she was already dead or not when someone left her body out there."

"How do you know all this?" Sylvia asked. The eyes of the others all indicated a similar desire to know how a stranger to town would have the inside scoop so quickly.

"I was at the little cafe yesterday when it all went down. As I drove here today, a police officer who worked the scene yesterday recognized me and asked me to identify the girl. They thought she was the one who was at the coffee shop. I recognized her."

No one said anything for a minute. "Are you a policeman?" Lynn asked.

"No. I used to be an investigator in the military, but now I'm retired."

"NCIS?" the cattle rancher with the red hair asked.

"No, with the air force, not the navy. I think Tom would rather not discuss the girl's death. I'm sure seeing the body was hard on him, and the incident put a damper on his big day."

"Yeah, I know he planned on having a lot more people," said a short elderly guy, whom everyone referred to as Doc. He used to have a family practice clinic in Johnson City. I didn't know his connection to Tom and Brenda. He had also come by himself.

"Whew, my momma always told me caffeine can kill you.

That's why I don't drink coffee. Okay. Well, let's not talk about it anymore," Lynn said.

I considered her comment about caffeine crass, but it did result in people breaking up into small groups of three or four again. Sylvia approached me. "An investigator? That must have been interesting."

"It had its moments, but for the most part it wasn't that interesting."

"I bet," she said like she didn't believe me. "Is that where you met Tom and Brenda?"

"In the air force, yes. We shared a couple of assignments together."

"Where's home?"

"Currently, it's Clovis, New Mexico."

"Currently?" she asked.

"Well, all my life I've been moving around every few years. Been in Clovis five years now. I don't have any real plans to move, but every now and then, I do get the bug. This is great country down here."

"It sure is. I have a number of clients along this stretch of 290 and one more a little south by Driftwood."

"Driftwood, sounds like a town in a cowboy movie. Is it a real place?" I asked.

"Sure is. More so than Luckenbach, made famous by the song, but which is only a few buildings nowdays."

"Do you just handle local wines?" I asked.

"Mostly. I'd do more, but the market is saturated with distributors. That's why I work my little piece of the world hard," she said. "I'm my own boss and have about a half dozen employees, depending on the season."

"I take it you're going to be taking care of Tom and Brenda?"

"Yes. I know I can get them in several restaurants and a few stores. Getting them into the larger stores takes a lot of work, but I've been pretty lucky in the Texas market," she said.

"Sounds like they're lucky to have you," I said.

"I'll do my best for them. How about you, Jim? Besides the past friendship, do you have any other business connection with Tom and Brenda?"

"No, like I said, just old friends. Receiving the invite surprised me. We hadn't communicated much in the past five years."

"Why's that?"

"No real reason, I'm just not much of a writer or a caller." It dawned on me that the real reason was that my ex did all the Christmas cards and other correspondence. Since our divorce, I hadn't changed my habits. I simply lost the person that took care of all the family correspondence.

"Oh, don't look so serious. It's really none of my business anyway," she said misinterpreting my thoughts. "Well, since I'm prying anyway, are you married, Jim?"

"Once," I said. "I guess I wasn't very good at it."

"How long were you married?"

"Twenty years. How about you?"

"Engaged twice. Both times we never made it to the altar."

"Same guy?" I said. The thought that the wine must be loosening our lips a little crossed my mind. We were both prying now.

"No," she said and started giggling. "That would be sad. No, the first was right out of college, and I think his parents bribed him out of the engagement. He was from a well to do

Boston family. I don't think they wanted a "hick" in the family."

"Too bad for him," I said. She smiled at my comment.

"The second was just earlier this year. A week before our wedding date, I found out he was sleeping with a woman he worked with. He told me to get over it, that it was no big deal. Looking back, I don't understand why I ever agreed to marry that jerk."

"Well, you know what they say, the third--"

"Don't even say it. Everyone has told me that! I don't think I even want to get married anymore."

"Okay, let's talk about something else," I said. "Why did you want to know if I had some other type connection with Tom and Brenda?"

"Sylvia," Brenda called from the door to the house. "Could you give me a hand with something?"

"Sure," Sylvia said and scurried away.

I watched Sylvia as she left me. I liked the look of the sky blue blouse on her, and not because it had a tight fit like Lynn's. The color of the shirt seemed perfect for her. Sylvia had fine, black hair that fell straight down a little past her shoulders. She didn't seem to be wearing much makeup. She had a slight natural coloring to her skin which made me wonder if she might be part American Indian. I'd put her in her early thirties, but I'd also give myself a substantial margin of error. Maybe five feet six or seven inches; my only criticism of her would be she needed to eat more. She didn't look unhealthily thin, but she would be more attractive with a little more weight on her.

The smell of barbecued ribs surged onto the deck. The hint of it had been there all day, but now it no longer teased us.

Sylvia came out carrying a tray of paper plates and napkins, and Tom followed her with a large platter of ribs. Everyone swarmed around them. I joined the crowd. While many of us ate a lot of appetizers to be polite due to the lack of other guests, our assault on the barbeque ribs came from sheer appreciation of how delicious they were. I felt like asking Tom if they had been catered, but he finally looked like something had gone right for him, so I didn't.

Chapter 3

"Tim, I appreciate your coming and spending the day with us," Tom said. Everyone else had gone. We stood on the deck and watched the last car drive away.

"My pleasure. This was fun, and I enjoyed seeing both of you again."

"This wasn't the day we had planned, but I think it turned out pretty good," Brenda said.

"I liked it," I said. "I'm no wine expert, but I enjoyed hearing about the process you go through to produce the wine."

"More importantly," Tom said, "did you really like the wine? No bull, what did you think?"

"I really liked them all. Like I said, I admit I'm no expert, and I doubt if I could tell a Merlot from a Cab without being told, but I liked what I tasted."

"Tom, we like the wine, and we think we're experts," Brenda said. "You need to quit doubting. Sylvia said she'll get us some feedback from her customers. Until that happens, we need to quit worrying about how the wine tastes. There's nothing we can do now anyway."

"She's right, Tom. By the way, you didn't try to sell any wine to us today," I said.

"That wouldn't have been appropriate," he said.

"I'd like to take some back with me."

"You can just have some," Brenda said. "Later, if you want more, we can ship you some."

"No, no, I don't want to be given anything. Let me buy a case of wine."

"Okay, okay," Tom said. "When are you going back to New Mexico?"

"Well, I kind of got roped into seeing some of the real estate around here tomorrow, so probably Monday."

"Is Sylvia showing you around?" Brenda asked.

"Yes."

"Oh good," she said with a conspiratorial grin.

"Oh, Brenda," Tom said. "Why--"

"Don't worry about Jim," Brenda cut in. "I'm sure he can take care of himself."

I stayed a few minutes longer before heading back to the hotel. Tom walked me out to my car.

"You must have spent a lot of time researching an operation like this before jumping in. How did you ever learn all this?" I motioned with my arms in an effort to encompass his entire operation.

"I've been interested in having my own winery for at least a decade. Two years before we moved down here, I volunteered at a winery in Maryland. I read a lot about the subject and took a couple of classes, too."

"Still it must have cost a fortune."

"You're telling me. I have a loan that I could've used to buy one of these luxury yachts. Don't think I haven't thought about it either."

"There's got to be a few quasi government programs here in Texas that could help you," I said.

"There are. I'm on a first name basis with the local Texas Cooperative Extension and the Texas Wine and Grape Growers Association. Don't think we just jumped blindly into this. We did an extensive risk assessment tailored specifically for starting a winery. As I mentioned earlier, right now we have to buy the bulk of the grapes we use, and like a lot of other places, we use a lot of juice in making our wine. Our goal is to ultimately be self-sufficient, although we will always bring in juice."

"I don't mean to imply you jumped in blindly."

"I know," Tom said. "And I didn't mean to infer that you did. I actually met Sylvia via phone before we even moved down here. She answered a lot of my questions. She also put me in touch with Theo. As you might have noticed, he thinks he's an expert on all things wine." He smiled when he said this. He realized that I thought Theo had sounded a little pompous. "The truth is that he is rather intelligent, and unlike going to other vintners for advice, which could be risky, Theo has no turf to protect. In fact, for a very small cash contribution he is a very small owner of this operation. So he's even more motivated to help out now."

"Did Lynn help you find this location?"

"Oh no, we didn't meet her until we came down here. She knew the prior owners who were listing the property. The location was part of the risk assessment."

"It's all fascinating. I'm impressed. I really am. Very few people would have the energy, much less the nerve, to do what you have done."

"Our kids were more terrified about it than we are. I guess they still are. They envision their inheritance going down the drain," Tom said. "Both have been down ostensibly to help out, but I'm pretty sure they just wanted to know if we had gone totally bonkers."

"I bet you'll do fine," I said despite my own doubts.

"The grapes we're growing won't be fully productive for a

few more years."

"When you walked us around, I didn't see a bottling place here."

"I don't know if we'll ever have our own bottling machinery," Tom said. "There's a guy that has a mobile unit. It's a big eighteen wheeler that he brings right to you. Fascinating thing to watch. He does the whole process."

"I never heard of such a thing."

"It's actually common nowadays for smaller and new wineries to contract out the bottling service."

"I have to admit, Tom, you've taught me a lot today."

"More importantly, did you like the wine?" he asked again.

"Hey! How many times do I have to tell you?" I grabbed his left shoulder. "Your wine is superb."

"Sorry, sorry. It's just that when push comes to shove, that's what really counts. By next year, we plan to have an actual tasting room in a separate building to accommodate tourists and special events."

"You have a lot more energy than I do," I said.

When I drove off, I noticed one lone sheriff's sedan parked at the crime scene. Police tape still marked off a wide patch of land around where the body was discovered. I didn't slow down, but the guilt of not doing anything when the poor girl was being dragged out of the coffee shop wormed its way back into my mind.

Later in bed at the hotel, I tried to focus my thoughts on Tom and Brenda and their start up vineyard. Despite my constant reassurances to him, I didn't think their chances of being successful were too good. Their wine tasted fine, but they had so much competition. I figured Sylvia would do her best to help them break into the local market, but they needed to go statewide and beyond.

Despite my efforts to not dwell on what I could've done to save the young woman, once sleep came, my dreams led me back to her. In my dream I saw her floating in the hotel pool. Our eyes met, and she smiled. Suddenly, she looked terrified and stretched a hand out to me for help. Something hidden from my sight under the water grabbed her and pulled her downward. I tried to get out of my lounge chair, but the straps in the chair kept tangling themselves around me holding me down. I fought and fought the chair. I looked around for someone else but saw no one. I knew her survival depended on me. Her eyes pleaded with me to do something. In the end, however, I could do nothing but sit there and watch her go under the water never to return to the surface.

A phone rang too loudly and too close to my head. I reached for it with mixed emotions. The clock said it wasn't quite six in the morning, too early to be rousted out of bed by a phone call. Yet the hotel phone had rescued me from my dream, and for that I was thankful.

"Yeah," I said into the phone. At the same time, I tried to work the fog out of my mind.

"Mr. West?"

"That's me. Who's this?"

"Sir, I'm Officer Creighton with the Fredericksburg police. I'm in the lobby of your hotel. I'm sorry sir, but we need your assistance for a few minutes."

"Right now?" I asked. My left eyelid didn't seem to want to stay open.

"Yes. Right now, if you don't mind."

"What in the world can you need me for at this time of the day on a Sunday?"

"Please sir, I was asked to get you, and told not to discuss the details of the investigation with you."

For a brief second I thought the police had come to arrest me, but that didn't make sense for a lot of reasons. I hadn't done anything to implicate myself in their investigation.

"Oh yeah, Mr. West," Officer Creighton said.

"Yes?"

"The Lieutenant told me to tell you that you're not in any trouble. He just needs your help again."

"Okay. I'll be down in a second."

Five minutes later, a very young looking Officer Creighton drove me into the parking lot behind a small warehouse. A single light illuminated the back of the small warehouse but did little for the large parking lot. I saw several police vehicles parked against the chain link fence at the back of the lot. Their flashers were not on. Two powerful, mobile lights lit up an area by the fence on the other side of the police cars. I didn't like any of the possible reasons they needed me here.

A tall, serious looking policewoman approached my side of the car as we came to a stop.

"Mr. West?" she asked once I got out of the car.

"Yes, what's up?"

"The Lieutenant thought you might be our quickest help," she said.

The Lieutenant again. I figured the Fredericksburg police must have only one or two lieutenants. I knew who they meant, even though they never said his name. The policewoman, who might have been in her thirties, looked exhausted. Her brown hair needed washing. Pulled back in a pony tail, part of it had come loose and hung down on the side of her face.

"Follow me, please."

I started to ask what was going on but didn't. I would see for myself in a minute. She took me through a gate in the fence and to the circle of police officers.

"Jim," Lieutenant Martin called to me as I approached. "I'm sorry to trouble you again, but we have another body for you to take a look at."

"What?" I asked. I don't know why I asked it. I knew what they wanted me for as soon as I saw the crime scene, but I did wonder why me. That would have been the better question.

"The guy who snatched the girl the other day. You told us you could recognize him again if you saw him. Remember?"

"He's dead, too?" I asked.

"Been that way all night."

"Good," the word jumped out. I didn't regret saying it.

"Here, take a look," the Lieutenant said. The crowd around the body opened to give me access.

"That's him," I said. Someone had shot him at close range in the right temple and the bullet went through his head and came out his left temple. The shot caused some distortion of his face, but I recognized him. I also noticed that on the back of his left hand he had a spider web tattoo. I remembered the young policeman interviewing me and asking me about his hands. One or more of the witnesses at the coffee shop must have seen the tattoo.

"Did you see anyone else at the coffee shop or the parking lot who might have known these two?"

"No, not at all," I said.

"In the statements we gathered, everyone mentioned that this guy accused our female victim of having someone else there. Did she make eye contact with anyone?"

"Sorry, Lieutenant, but like I said before, I thought she was alone. Do you know who this guy is?"

"We know he wasn't her husband. She wasn't married."

"How about the ring?"

"Belonged to her mother who passed away a year ago. Cancer," he said as an afterthought as though it made a difference. "Miss Wilikin has worn it ever since."

"Think she was running from this guy?" I asked.

"Maybe. The guy had no ID on him. The van had been stolen Thursday in Austin."

The coffee shop incident happened on Friday.

"Everything happened quickly. He tracked her down fast, unless she was involved with the car theft and was traveling with him."

"She wasn't. Found the car she was driving in the strip mall parking lot next to the coffee shop. Had her suitcase and backpack in it," the Lieutenant said.

"What was she doing here in Fredericksburg?" I asked.

He looked at me. Maybe a light bulb went on in his tired mind and reminded him that I wasn't part of the investigating team. "Creighton!" He called to the young officer who had driven me here.

"Yes sir," Officer Creighton said from the other side of the fence.

"Drive Mr. West back to his hotel. When you get back, I want you over here watching and learning."

Creighton drove me back. He appeared to be embarrassed

by the Lieutenant's remarks.

"You never really get used to them, you know," I said.

"What?" he asked.

"The dead ones. You just have to come up with your own way of handling them, so they don't totally mess up your mind."

"First the girl and now him," he said. "They're my first two like that. I had to respond to an old woman who had a heart attack. That wasn't too bad."

"Homicides are always the worst," I said.

"I heard you were a criminal investigator in the military. How was that?" he asked.

"I enjoyed it," I said. They had done a background check on me. I guess it made sense. Most of the customers at the coffee shop were probably locals. That made me the stranger.

The first hint of dawn lit up the sky in the east when Officer Creighton dropped me off at the hotel. I debated whether or not I should get some breakfast or go back to bed. I had a few hours before Sylvia would come and get me. Two young kids screaming at each other and running around the now crowded breakfast area made my decision easy for me. I returned to my room.

Perhaps seeing the guy who had kidnapped and likely killed the girl now dead gave me some morbid comfort. Whatever the reason, I fell right into a deep sleep. Once again the shrill ring of the hotel phone yanked me out of my slumber.

"Jim?" Sylvia asked. "I'm here."

"Oh, sorry," I said. "Crazy night. I'll be right down."

"Are you okay?"

"Yeah, I'll explain when I get down there."

I took a little longer to clean up than I had for Officer Creighton. Women have that effect on me. I found her in the breakfast room drinking a cup of coffee. She was the only person in the room. The breakfast food, plates, and utensils had been removed, but the coffee pots were still available.

"Good morning," I said.

"Grab a cup of coffee, if you want," she said.

I did. "Sorry I overslept, but I do have an excuse," I said as I sat down opposite her at the small table.

"Oh, that's no problem. We're not in a rush. Have you had breakfast?"

"No, it's been an odd day."

"Odd or not, I have a favorite bakery-slash-café that I'd like to take you to before we start looking at some property," she said.

"Sounds good, but I'm not sure what kind of company I'll be today."

"Oh, don't worry, I'm not a realtor. I won't be trying to sell you anything. I hope one day to have a nice piece of land for myself."

"I know we're just doing this for fun, but something is going to be troubling me all day, so let me tell you how my day got started."

She looked at me with that half curious and half concerned look people get. I explained how the police had come to the hotel and had me view the body of the man who shot the coffee shop employee and took the young woman.

"My God, did you know the man?" she asked.

"No, but the police knew I could identify him as the man who did the shooting and kidnapped that young woman. I don't think they know who he is yet."

"Why did they pick on you rather than someone else?"

"Very good question," I said. "I think the main reason is that yesterday they had me look at the young woman. That was a coincidence. I happened to be driving to Tom and Brenda's, and as I passed the crime scene, Lieutenant Martin saw me and stopped me. Since they used me once, I guess to them it made sense to use me again."

"You said that was the main reason. Is there another?" she asked.

I hesitated for a second. I didn't want to get into a big conversation about my past.

"I have a law enforcement background. They've learned that from their background check on me and probably felt that I would be more willing to help than someone else might."

"That's right, you said you were a cop."

"No, like I mentioned yesterday, I think, I wasn't exactly a police officer. I was a special agent with the Air Force Office of Special Investigations for twenty years."

"Two specials in one sentence, I guess that makes you--"

"Don't say it," I said.

"Okay," she said with a grin that indicated the word special might jump out at any second. "Let's go eat a late breakfast."

We left the hotel. She had dressed casual, but in her jeans, pressed white blouse, and fancy boots, she outclassed me. She drove a big, blue Ford Expedition. It had its share of dents and scratches.

"My old reliable," she said. "Has over a hundred thousand miles on it and it's only five years old. I can put over twenty cases of wine back there." She gestured with her head to the space behind her. The back seats had all been placed in the down position making the space behind the front seats flat.

"Makes sense."

"A lot of my male friends have tried to talk me into a pickup, and there are a lot of pickup trucks I like. However, there's a lot of dust and just enough rain here in this area to make delivering a dozen cases of wine to someone in the rain not something I want to do in a pickup." She gave me a defensive look.

"No argument from me," I said.

"It's either this or a van," she said and turned into a small parking lot. We parked in front of a building painted a light blue and boasting a sign that identified the place as Emma's World Finest Café.

The name sounded off, like an apostrophe s needed to be placed at the end of the word world, or maybe finest wasn't a word. Something sounded odd about the name, but perhaps they wanted a quirky name.

"Is it?" I asked.

"Absolutely."

The word hadn't gotten out. The place had a dozen tables, and only one other table was occupied. We grabbed a table by the front window.

"Hey, girl, how's everything?" A very tall blond approached our table. "What do you all want to drink this morning?"

"Hi, Barb. We're doing well. How's business?"

"Not too bad earlier, I think the flyers you took to the hotels might be paying off. Coffee?"

We both agreed to coffee, and Barb strolled off.

"A friend?" I asked. She looked to be around Sylvia's age.

"Yeah, Barb's really sweet. I met her here a couple of years ago."

An older looking version of Sylvia appeared in the hallway that I assumed led back to the kitchen and offices.

"I wondered when you'd show up. When you said breakfast, I thought you meant before noon," the woman said.

"Oh, Mom, it's not even noon yet," Sylvia said. "Mom, this is Jim West. Jim, this is my mother, Emma."

"Nice to meet you, Emma. I'm looking forward to what I understand is an excellent breakfast." She had the same cute smile as her daughter. I guessed she had to treat her hair to keep it as black as Sylvia's, and she carried a few more pounds than her daughter. In my mind, that was a plus. I guessed she was only five to ten years older than me.

"You're not from around here, are you?" Emma asked.

"No. I came down from Clovis, New Mexico, for the opening of the Broken Spur Vineyards."

"So, you two met at the opening?"

"Yes, Mother. Jim's interested in looking at some property around here, so I'm driving him around today."

"I would think Lynn would like to do that," Emma said.

Her tone indicated to me she might be teasing her daughter.

"I think we're ready to order, please," Sylvia said.

"Have you seen a menu yet?" Emma asked me. Her grin hadn't disappeared, so whatever she had said to irritate Sylvia, hadn't affected her own cheerfulness.

"Not yet," I said.

Just then, Barb reappeared with our coffee, water, and menus.

Emma gave Sylvia a friendly pat on her shoulders and disappeared down the hallway.

I ordered eggs, sausage, and a cinnamon roll. Sylvia ordered a fruit dish and toast.

"Sorry about my mom."

"What do you mean? I thought she was nice," I said.

"You would think once I hit thirty, she'd ease up on me."

"I guess it's hard for any of us to change our ways."

"You catch that comment about Lynn? You know Lynn Brooks, the realtor who was at the opening?" Sylvia asked.

"Yes, but I don't know what she meant by it."

"Well, Lynn has issues. She has never met a man she didn't like."

"Is that bad?" I asked.

"That's not what I mean. First, she's married, but that doesn't stop her from chasing other men. I can't imagine that her husband doesn't know about it."

"Think he doesn't care?"

"Who knows?" she said. "Twice I started relationships only to have Lynn steal them away."

"That's not good."

"Oh, it wasn't that big of a deal at the time. My involvement with the men hadn't gone that far. It just frustrated me that they left me to have a fling with a married woman. I made the mistake of mentioning it to Mom, and she's turned it into a bigger deal than it was."

"I think she may just be picking on you for fun."

"No. She's worried that I won't find someone to marry. So, anytime I show up with a man anywhere, she's right there to remind me that I better set the hook before someone else like

Lynn steals him away."

"You might want to tell her that I'm just passing through," I said.

"It doesn't matter. Her comments weren't directed at you. She's really a great mom and nice to everyone. It's just my relationship with men, or lack of, that she feels a need to micro-manage."

"Guess you have to let time solve that one," I said and wondered if that made any sense at all.

"How about you? Did you say yesterday you were married once?" she asked.

"Yes."

"Is it worth it? My mom puts a lot more value in it than I do."

"I guess it is to most people, but definitely not everyone. It's more work than advertised. For most it's a series of compromises, and I've heard that more than half of all married couples end up getting a divorce."

"You sound a little negative on it."

"I don't know," I said. "I don't want to be, but my divorce took a lot out of me."

"Financially?"

"No." I didn't say anything else about it, and she had the sense not to pursue it. For the most part, I had finally put it behind me. I'd like to keep it there.

"Should I marry for money or love?" she asked.

"Now that's a good question? I'd say love, but hope the money is there."

"Mom would agree with you, but maybe I'm getting cynical. I've been working hard for years and am barely staying afloat.

Same with this café and my mom. If I get to pick whom I can marry, then I'm going to pick a rich one," she said.

"A cold, calculating woman," I said in jest.

"Damn straight. Are you rich?"

"I wish."

The food came, and the huge cinnamon roll took my attention away from our conversation about marriage. For a few minutes we both ate in silence.

"If the man you saw today, you know, the dead man, killed that woman, who do you think killed him?"

"That's the big question the police will be trying to solve."

"A love triangle?" Sylvia asked.

"Could be if the guy was her boyfriend. I can't see the attraction to him."

"You don't have to. In fact, she may not have been attracted to him. It only had to be in his mind."

"That's true," I said.

"So maybe her true lover killed him for revenge."

"I think you have romance on the brain today."

"Well, could my theory be possible?" she asked.

"Yes, it's definitely possible."

Our conversation stayed lighthearted for the rest of our breakfast. Sylvia grew on me. It must have been her personality more than her looks. I mean, she was attractive enough, but all she ate was fruit. She put a calorie-free sweetener in her coffee. Every time she opened her mouth to put in a blueberry or a small bite of cantaloupe, I wanted to jump across the table and stuff a chunk of my cinnamon roll into it.

Chapter 4

Sylvia showed me seven or eight small ranches. She referred to them as ranchettes. Two of them really appealed to me, but their cost, each at a million plus, turned them into one of those things I might buy if I ever won the lottery.

We said our goodbyes at three in the afternoon. I promised to look her up the next time I came to Fredericksburg. I was half serious. I probably would return at some point and more than likely give her a call if I did. She was nice, and I enjoyed being with her. She couldn't be characterized as one of those women who captivated you from the first moment you saw her. However, I imagined she could also be thinking the same thing about me.

I hadn't exactly been a dating machine since my divorce. At first, I had been demoralized and emotionally damaged. That baggage is mostly in my past, I think, but my relationships with women have remained short and sporadic. While I believe a steady, serious relationship could finally "fix" me, I knew I hadn't been trying too hard to find one.

I needed to say good bye to Tom and Brenda and pick up the case of wine I purchased. They had offered it to me free, but I insisted on buying it. After I heard the price, I wished I had taken them up on their free offer.

I arrived at the Hasbens' house and rang their doorbell at five minutes past three. No one answered, so I walked around the house to see if I could find them outside. They knew I'd be showing up around three and said they'd be here all day. I heard voices coming from one of the out buildings. As I approached I could tell that the voices belonged to Tom and Brenda, and the tone of their conversation wasn't pleasant.

"Tom!' I shouted like I didn't know where they were. "Hey, Tom!"

He appeared in the doorway to the building that he had described yesterday as the garage for his tractor and other equipment. Brenda walked by him toward me.

"Hey, Jim, let me get that case of wine for you," she said as she passed me. It looked like she might have been crying.

"Did I come at a bad time?" I asked Tom.

"No. Her friend Lynn, and I do mean her friend Lynn, not mine, sent me a text a little while ago. We had discussed the purchase of another twenty acres to the south. Just a discussion, mind you; I've never given Lynn any indication that I really want to do it."

"Didn't Brenda know about the possibility?"

"Oh sure, we've discussed it. That's not the problem." He hesitated for a second like he was considering what to tell me.

"Hey, it's none of my business. You don't have to tell me anything."

"It's not that. It's just …. It's just a little weird. I didn't even catch it. Brenda did, and now she thinks I'm involved somehow with Lynn."

Sylvia's comments about Lynn, something I had already deleted from the ever shrinking part of my mind where I try to only keep significant facts, leaped back into my mind.

"Why would she think that?" I asked.

"Look at this text and tell me how she got the idea." He held out his cell phone and pulled up the text.

I read the text. It didn't contain anything personal. It consisted of a short paragraph detailing the land's dimensions and provided her estimate for what he could buy the land. It ended with a link to her website.

"What do you think?" Tom asked.

"I don't understand," I said.

"That's how I felt when Brenda started going off on me. Would you have clicked on her website?"

"No. If I had any questions I would have called her or sent her a text."

"Well, women obviously don't think like we guys do," he said.

"That I do know."

"I mentioned the text to Brenda, and she asked if she could read it. Hell, I said sure and gave her the phone. Next thing I know I'm in the doghouse."

I took the phone again and clicked on the link to the website. A video of Lynn popped up. Taken in dim lighting, I had to squint to see much, but it was fairly obvious that the video displayed a naked Lynn Brooks lying face down on her bed. The camera angle focused at her head while she looked up into the camera, so in reality you don't see much. I considered the pose more of a tease than anything else.

"Hey, Tom, if you do go through with this next purchase, I want to offer you a signing bonus. You'll like this one more than the last one," Lynn said into the camera before everything goes blank.

"You've got to be kidding," I said.

"I didn't even see that before Brenda showed it me. She wants to know what the first signing bonus was that Lynn referred to."

"Well?"

"There wasn't any. I mean nothing at all like what she's implying now." Tom shook his head in frustration. "After I signed the last form at her office to buy this property, she gave me a hug and a kiss on the cheek. That did kind of surprise me at the time, but that's all there was."

"Did Brenda see it?"

"No. We had already signed everything. At least we thought we had. We were at the mall getting a few things, and I got a call from Lynn. She said she overlooked one form that needed a signature and told me that Brenda didn't need to sign the form, just me. I told Brenda to continuing shopping and I would run back to Lynn's office to sign the form."

"So she thinks something may have happened between you and Lynn when you went back to her office without her?" I asked.

"Yes, or maybe later, I don't know. She did offer to go to Lynn's office with me, but I told her she should stay at the mall. Of course, that's what she remembers," Tom said.

"Nothing happened. She'll get over it," I said.

"Tom!" Brenda shouted from the back door of the house.

"Yeah, honey, what can I do for you?"

"You never put the Black Velvet in the case for Jim."

"Oh yeah, I meant to get that last night. I'll go get it right now."

"Don't worry about it," I said. "Just throw in whatever you have at the house."

"No, no. The Black Velvet is our best wine. We've got plenty of it. I'll go get it." He left me standing there at the entrance to the garage. I felt a little awkward and was about to start following him when Brenda called me.

"Tom, come on in here. There's no use you getting yourself all dirty in there."

"Okay," I said and went into the house with her.

"Did you hear us fighting out there?" she asked. The tears I thought I saw earlier had disappeared.

"Not really," I said.

"You two get a good laugh at me?"

"What? No, no way. Tom's upset about all this as much as you." I knew as soon as I said it that I had probably been tricked into saying more than I should have.

"So, he did discuss it with you." She said it with a slight hint of triumph in her voice that she had gotten me to admit it.

"Yes, Brenda, he did, and he swore to me that there has never been anything between Lynn and him."

"People just don't send videos of themselves like that," she said.

"Oh, believe me, they do."

"I wish I could believe you."

"I've only been here a couple of days, but one thing I learned before all this," I motioned with my hand toward the garage, "was that your friend Lynn--"

"She's no longer my friend."

"Was," I continued, "that Lynn, despite being married, likes to pursue men, even married men."

"She might be the aggressor, but Tom doesn't have the best record in not touching, either."

"Brenda, I'm not the right person to confide in. I'm no expert, and I don't need to hear all this." Where was Tom and that wine, I wondered. I wanted to leave before I got sucked deeper into this conflict.

"You probably knew her, you know."

"No, Brenda, I didn't know anything, and I'd rather not know anything."

She ignored me. She needed to vent, and I was stuck there.

"It was that sergeant in his office who used to go on those trips with him. You know the one. She had the frizzy hair and bad teeth."

I couldn't remember who used to work with Tom at the Pentagon. I also felt Brenda's description might be a little prejudiced.

"Before you go too ballistic on Tom, Brenda, go buy Sylvia a cup of coffee and have her tell you about Lynn."

She looked at me with a look that indicated that I had made her remember something. "Why Sylvia?" she asked.

"First, she's known Lynn a lot longer than you, and second, although please don't tell her I told you, she's had a few experiences with Lynn hitting on her boyfriends."

"Boyfriends? What are we talking about? High school?"

"No," I said.

"You really are behind the times, Jim," she said. "What did you think of Sylvia?"

The question caught me off guard, but at least she changed the subject.

"I liked her. We had a nice time."

"I admire her," Brenda said.

"Brenda," Tom entered through the back door. "The key to the room is missing. Have you seen it?"

"Right there," she pointed to the coffee table next to the door.

He grabbed the keys and with a look of frustration, left.

"She said she had a nice time, too," Brenda said.

"Sylvia?" I asked. My mental focus was way off center. I was still trying to figure out the look on Tom's face.

"Of course, unless you're seeing Lynn, too."

"Come on, Brenda."

"I'm sorry, Jim. I shouldn't take this out on you."

"Oh, I understand." Of course, I didn't understand any of it. I simply wanted to leave.

"You know we've been married for almost twenty-one years. This," she raised both hands to indicate the house and property, "was our twentieth anniversary gift to ourselves. We put our life savings into it and borrowed a lot more. I can't afford to divorce him, but you tell him if I do catch him fooling around on me again, I'll cut his balls off." She went outside through the back door and left me in the house alone.

"I'm sorry about all this," Tom said a minute later. He entered the house carrying a bottle of red wine.

"My bad timing," I said.

"Why would Lynn send me a text like that?" he asked.

"I hear she's got a bad habit of going after a lot of men," I said. I may have stretched what I heard a little, but I didn't think it mattered.

"Did she hit on you, too?" he asked.

"No, but I've only been here two days. Give me time."

"You know Brenda sent me out after the Black Velvet even though she knew the keys to the room were here, not in the warehouse where we keep them. She probably brought the keys in here when she returned with the rest of the wine just to harass me."

"She's pissed," I said. "I told her there was no way you had any interest in Lynn."

"Thanks, buddy. The truth is I didn't."

"Didn't or don't."

"You saw the video. She all but said come and get me. I'd be lying if I didn't admit that that got me a little interested," Tom said.

I couldn't argue. I'd had the urge to ask if I could watch it again.

"Tom, be warned. Brenda said if she caught you fooling around with Lynn she'd cut off a couple things you'd rather not lose. I don't think she was kidding."

He grimaced at the idea. "Don't worry, I won't. This place will keep me more than busy. We've got everything invested in this place. I'm not going to blow it."

"Good." My cell phone rang. I didn't recognize the number.

"Go ahead and take it," Tom said.

I walked off a few paces and took the call.

"Any problems?" Tom asked after I hung up.

"Yes. That was the police. They want me to come in there tomorrow morning to look at a couple of photos."

"Why?"

"I'm not sure. I hope I can convince them tomorrow that I have nothing more to contribute. I'd like to go back home tomorrow."

"Is this related to the dead girl?" Tom asked.

"Yes."

"Such a shame."

"Yes, it is," I said.

I drove back into Fredericksburg wondering how so much

trouble could find a small town like this. My mind wasn't on my driving, but the Mustang knew its way to the hotel by now.

I knew a little about Fredericksburg. It's been around since the mid 1800's, and, like many towns in south central Texas, was established by German immigrants. Although their settlement was situated on the Comanche frontier, they made a treaty with the tribes that somehow endured the years.

Although barely half the size of Clovis, New Mexico, the place I now called home, Fredericksburg seemed to have much more to offer. I knew a lot of the attractions were actually located in the surrounding areas, but Fredericksburg seemed to be the perfect staging point to see them all. However, I knew I might be a little biased in my feelings. While driving around in the small city earlier, I had discovered both a Fredericksburg Brewing Company and a Fredericksburg Winery. The city planners definitely deserved a pay raise.

Chapter 5

"We're trying to determine if any of these men were at the coffee shop when the shooting and kidnapping occurred," said the tall policewoman who I had seen at the site where the dead man had been found. She didn't look as worn out as she did at that crime scene, and her brown hair looked a lot better. We almost looked eye to eye, but I thought she might be an inch or so shorter than me. I also thought she could be a runner. She appeared to be in great physical shape. This time her uniform included a name tag that identified her as Morris.

"You mean the two men who left before the police arrived?" I asked. I thought it had to be those two they were interested in, since they had the names of everyone who had remained.

"Yes, both or either."

I looked at the eight photographs she displayed in front of me. "Are these from the security cameras?" I asked.

"Yes."

"They aren't very good," I said while I studied the pictures.

"That's all we have at the moment," she said with a slight irritation in her voice.

"I can't say for sure, but I think these two were the guys that slipped out right after the incident occurred." I pointed to two of the photographs. "I'm pretty sure one of the guys wore that red and grey plaid shirt. I'm more sure of that than the faces of either."

"Thanks. Did they say anything before they left?"

"No. The manager shouted at them to stay. I did too, but

they left. I thought they just didn't want to get involved. Are you all thinking something else?"

"We're simply working all the angles, Mr. West."

"Please call me Jim. I'm not that old." I doubted that I had more than a dozen years on her.

She looked at me like she was thinking who was I trying to kid.

"Come on, how old are you?" I asked.

That got a smile out of her normally serious face. She looked a lot prettier when she smiled. Most people do.

"Wait here for a minute, please. I need to talk to the Lieutenant before I set you free."

She walked out of the small interview room. I figured if one could get through the tough veneer of hers, you would find a pleasant person trying to get out. She returned a minute later.

"That was quick," I said.

"We're going to try to locate these two guys. They paid with cash, and the staff at the coffee shop has already told us they didn't know any of the guys in the photos. They had seen all of them more than once, so we believe they're local."

"Could be that Fredericksburg is on their route, and they have a habit of stopping at that coffee shop when they travel through," I said.

"That, too," she said.

"Guess you don't need my advice."

"If we do, we'll ask. In fact, the Lieutenant wants you to stick around until tomorrow. He considers you a material witness. Will you stay in Fredericksburg for the remainder of the day and check in tomorrow by phone?"

"Oh, come on. You can reach me by phone, fax, and email. I

only live a half day drive away."

"One more day?" she asked.

"Okay, okay, but that's all," I said. "You'll have to buy me dinner." I said it without any real forethought.

"No," she said like she didn't have to think about the answer either.

I left the station a little dejected, and not because I got turned down for dinner. I returned to the La Quinta. My stay had already been extended by one night. Nothing against the hotel, but I hoped it would be my last.

I didn't know what to do on a Sunday night in Fredericksburg, but I knew I didn't want to spend the evening sitting in my hotel room. I didn't mind watching a football game, but I'd rather do it from a sports bar.

The clerk at the front desk suggested the Rockbox Theater. I hadn't heard of it, but it sounded interesting. The clerks said it wasn't a bar, but he thought I could get a beer there. He further said that local talent performed a variety of entertainment that ranged from the golden era of rock and roll to family friendly comedy. On occasion, they had a big name performer or group, but he didn't think anyone special was performing at the moment. He did tell me the Rockbox was an indoor theater, and because it could seat nearly five hundred people, I didn't need reservations.

I drove away from the hotel looking for a Mexican restaurant I had seen earlier that day. The Rockbox Theater sounded interesting, but I thought I'd keep my evening plans simple.

I parked on the street about a block from the restaurant. The town still appeared to be full of life. When I got out of the car, I received a text message on my phone.

"Dinner tonite? Need to talk - Syl"

For a brief second, I thought Officer Morris had reconsidered my dinner request. I sent Sylvia a response. "Sure Where? When?" I figured in twenty years texting will have completely destroyed the English language.

Her return text said, "Seven at Vaudeville on Main. Downstairs."

That gave me a little over an hour. I returned to the hotel, showered, and watched part of an episode of Seinfeld. I'd seen it once or twice before, but it still made me laugh.

I got to Vaudeville a few minutes early so I checked out a granite and iron works store next door. The place was fascinating. On display were dozens of tables, desks, and counters made with granite tops and iron frames. One table that I really liked looked like it could easily seat eight people. It probably weighed more than my Mustang. I left the store before the temptation got too high.

Vaudeville wasn't what I expected. At street level I discovered a store. I double checked the sign out front and looked for the stairs that would lead down to the restaurant. Downstairs, I found a deep rectangular room. Wine bottles lined the walls at the bottom of the stairs. Sylvia hadn't arrived yet, so I grabbed a table in the center of the room and sat in a chair facing the stairs. At separate corners of the room, tables had been pulled together. Ten or so customers crowded around them in each corner. Both groups were loud. Three men sat at separate spots along the long counter bar, and one couple snuggled at a table in the far end of the room.

At ten minutes past seven, I started wondering if I had made a mistake. I checked my phone and discovered I had missed a text from Sylvia. "Delayed by ten minutes or so."

A server had come by shortly after I arrived, and I had asked him to come back in a few minutes. He hadn't returned, so I signaled to him.

"Sorry, sir. I thought you might be waiting for someone."

"I am, but she's been delayed a bit. How's this cheese and meat tray?" I asked and held up the small plastic frame that announced today's specials.

"Very good, sir. It's one of our top sellers."

"Let me have one, and do you carry any wines from the Broken Spur?"

"Broken Spur? I don't believe we do. I've never heard of it."

"You will. What's a good local wine?" I asked.

"I recommend a Becker Claret, sir." He answered so quickly, I figured he had been instructed on what to recommend by the management.

"Bring me a glass of that. Once my friend arrives, I'll let her make the choices. She's more of an expert than I am."

"Yes, sir, coming right up."

He wasn't kidding. In two minutes he returned with the wine and the tray of thinly sliced meats and cheeses. Sylvia appeared on the stairs as the server walked away. She had on the same clothes she had worn earlier in the day.

I stood and signaled to her. She saw me and smiled.

"Oh, that looks good," she said upon seeing the food on the table. "I'm starving."

"I didn't order anything for you to drink. I didn't know what you might be in the mood for."

"A glass of wine would be great, and a big glass of water."

"I asked for something from the Broken Spur, but they don't carry it."

"Yet," she said. "I haven't been able to get in here yet."

"We should go somewhere else," I said.

"No," she grinned. "I've got to keep schmoozing them."

"Ma'am, can I get you something to drink?" Our waiter must have seen her arrival and returned.

She turned to me. "What are you having?"

I had to look at the waiter.

"A Becker Claret," the waiter said.

"Okay, that's good. I'll have one of those, too."

"Should I get a bottle?" I asked her.

"Oh, no. That'll be too much. Also a glass of water, please."

The waiter walked off to get her glass of wine.

"Long time, no see," I said. No reason not to show off my great sense of humor.

"I know," she said. "You know who called me today and insisted on talking?"

"Brenda?"

"Yes."

"I hope you aren't mad," I said.

"No, not at all, but I could've been."

Something in my head told me not to ask her to explain.

"At first, I was a bit defensive with her, too. I certainly didn't want to get into my lousy love life, my mom, and Lynn with her. I quickly discovered, though, that she didn't want to know about me. She needed some reassurance and wanted to talk."

"She seemed a little desperate."

"Can you blame her? Did you see the video?"

"Yes." I started to say something more, but she continued talking.

"She showed it to me. Can you believe it?"

"I thought it was on Tom's phone."

"She brought his phone. She gave him hers. I think she plans on keeping his for a while in case something else comes in."

Poor Tom, I thought. I doubted that the phone exchange had been his idea.

"Can you believe the bitch?" she asked.

For a second I didn't know who she meant.

"She made a direct move on Tom to get him to do something that could break up his marriage." I was glad that Lynn was the bitch and not Brenda. "I wouldn't blame Brenda if she shot Lynn."

"Too many people have already been shot around here," I said, but I knew Sylvia had a point. Messing with another person's spouse has been a fatal mistake for a lot of people throughout history. I just hoped Brenda wouldn't do anything that crazy.

"Yeah, but could you blame her? You saw the video. I'd love to show it to my mother. How could any man find it sexy?"

I tried to look like I agreed with her, but that wasn't enough.

"Are you telling me that seeing that video would make you want to drive over there?" she asked even though I didn't say anything.

"No way," I said, but it was hard to keep a straight face.

"You rat. You'd go over there, wouldn't you?"

"No, I really wouldn't. She's married. I try to avoid affairs with married women."

"If she wasn't married?"

"Too many if's," I said. It was a silly conversation, but I answered. "If we were both single and unattached, what would it really matter one way or the other?"

"Okay, okay, but Brenda is concerned that Tom may have led her on or maybe that they've already done something together," Sylvia said.

"I know, but there hasn't been."

"How do you know?"

"He told me so. Secondly, he didn't check out the link, Brenda did. He didn't expect any hidden message," I said.

"You guys," she said shaking her head.

"We don't think like you. I know. I even read that book men are from Mars and women are from somewhere else. You know, Brenda jumped on me for siding with Tom, too."

"I'm not jumping on you, Jim. You were just at the wrong place and wrong time. She needed to let off some steam. She was still quite agitated when she got to me."

"I'm sorry that I mentioned you to her," I said.

"Just panicked, didn't you?" she said. Her grin had returned.

"Yes. I was cornered."

"Actually, I shouldn't say this, but what girl doesn't want to be a confidant?"

"You mean hear some gossip?" My turn to grin.

"Except this isn't gossip. It's real and confidential. I had to talk to someone, too," she said. "That's why I called you. You already know everything."

"Have you mentioned it to your mother?"

"Not yet. I'm not sure if I should. She has a group of friends that do a lot of gossiping."

"If word got around, maybe Lynn would start behaving," I said.

"No way. She loves the notoriety, and I wouldn't want to hurt Brenda. Too bad she can't go to the police with it."

"The police?" I asked.

"Yeah, like if it was against the law to text someone a picture like that."

"It was mostly suggestive. You couldn't really see anything. What I've been wondering is if she had someone take the video for her, or if she did it herself?"

"Like her husband?" Sylvia asked. Her eyebrows shot up. "Wouldn't that be something? I hadn't even thought about that!"

"Well, you said he almost had to know about her affairs. They may video a lot more of what she does."

She looked at me for a second. "Oh, don't go there. That's sick. This is a small town. We don't need to know about stuff like that."

"What does Brenda plan on doing now? Did she tell you?" I asked.

"Not really. She plans to keep Tom on a short leash and, like I said, she has his phone. I didn't get the impression that she was going to confront Lynn. At least, not yet."

"I guess they won't be doing any future business with her either."

"I'm sure they won't," she said.

"It surprises me that her reputation hasn't hurt her business," I said.

"Probably helps it."

"Hope you aren't getting any ideas how to expand your clientele."

"Ha! I don't have the body to be sending pictures of myself around." She didn't elaborate, and I didn't comment. I did make a face at her to indicate she was full of bull, but I also noticed she had only nibbled on a few slices of meat from the tray.

"Tom told me the two of you actually met via phone before their arrival down here."

"That's true. I was happy to snare a new client, even if that client hadn't even started an operation down here yet."

"Well, he claimed you were a lot of help to him," I said.

"Advice is easy and cheap," she said. "They had to take all the risk and do all the work."

"I hope they succeed," I said.

"It's a tough world. I suggested they start small to get a grasp on what it takes to simply get the business going. They can always refinance if they can show progress. They have a good business plan, and I have suggested which grape varieties can best survive and are marketable around here. There are a couple other small wineries in the area that are struggling. Without being too obvious, we're trying to use them as case studies on what not to do."

"You and Tom?"

"Actually more me and Brenda."

The restaurant filled up fairly quickly after Sylvia's arrival. The customers came in all shapes and sizes and in all sorts of attire. I thought that might be typical of a small town a little more than an hour away from a couple of the country's largest cities. Too far away from both San Antonio and Austin to be considered a suburb of either, Fredericksburg probably still had more than its share of transplanted urban elites. Slim customers in suits shared the room comfortably with obese customers in overalls and t-shirts.

The waiter returned, and Sylvia ordered a small salad with a flavored vinaigrette. I asked for some bread to go along with the meat and cheese tray. I had a feeling I would have to eat most of it myself. Luckily, I thought it was delicious.

It turned out I was right. Once her salad arrived, Sylvia nibbled on it for the rest of the evening and never touched the cheese or meat again. We ended up slowly eating and drinking for a couple of hours. We should have ordered that bottle of wine. It would've been considerably cheaper. She grew on me, and I apparently made an impression on her. By the end of the evening, I agreed to ride along on her rounds in the morning, and she agreed to spend the night with me at the hotel.

A beautiful full moon filled the clear sky.

Chapter 6

At nine that Monday morning, I stood in front of the La Quinta and waited for Sylvia's return. She had gone home to change and get whatever paperwork she needed. Optimistic, I checked out of the hotel. I couldn't imagine why I wouldn't be able to go home late today.

The Ford Expedition rolled into the parking lot and stopped in front of me.

"Hop in," Sylvia said.

I had already opened the door. "I can hop, you know," I said. I looked in the back of the vehicle. "Empty."

"Yeah, today I pick up from two of my producers and bring the wine to my warehouse. I also get requisition requirements from my purchasers. Those, however, come in electronically. If there are any emergency requests, I fill those today. Otherwise, I'll fill the purchase orders tomorrow afternoon. I'll also notify the producers of any changes to the usual weekly order."

"Sounds like you have this operation running smooth as silk."

"Ha! Nothing stays the same. It's hard to meet anyone's expectations, and it's way too easy to screw up."

"Well, you wouldn't have made it this far if you weren't doing a good job," I said.

"Thanks. You know, I've had customers call me at midnight saying they need more of this wine or that wine."

"You're kidding. They couldn't push a different wine on their customers?"

"You'd be surprised," she said. "For whatever reason, some

people want a specific wine and nothing else. And you know, I can't blame a lot of my customers. Many have their own fledgling businesses, just like me, that they're trying to keep afloat. They would do almost anything to keep their customers happy. They know I'm local and can get the wine to them in minutes. Often they'll send a runner to get it, so all I have to do is wake up and drive to the warehouse."

"I guess you have regular pick up days where you get the wine from the vineyards."

"Yes. Wednesday is my busiest day picking up wine. I'm literally going back and forth all day on Wednesday."

"No one to help you?" I asked.

"Oh, I have back up, but I do most of the vineyard runs. Jack and Trey deliver to most of the customers who buy the stuff. Either one of those can pick up from the producers if I can't. I stop by the restaurants and bars to schmooze with the buyers at least once a month, usually a lot more often."

"I take it you try to keep a steady inventory at your warehouse."

"Two weeks-worth of inventory, no more," she said. "I learned that the hard way. Learning how to shave my little piece out of the middle wasn't easy either. It's a fine balance."

"I imagine the seller knows what he needs to sell each bottle or case for to make a profit," I said.

She smiled. "That's something they all need to get their hands around or they won't last, but you're right. They learn what they need to make off every bottle they sell."

"And the restaurant owners want to buy the wine at the lowest cost they can," I said.

"Yep, and I'm not the only distributor around, so I play the seasonal factors the best I can."

"What do you mean?" We were now speeding east out of town toward Austin and Johnson City.

"Kind of my secret formula," she said.

I thought she'd elaborate. She didn't.

"We'll stop at Bee Winters' place first. You'll like her. She's one of a kind."

She turned south off the highway. I saw signs to Luckenbach, but before we got there we took a narrow, winding road off to the east. After a while, I noticed a small sign identifying our destination as Royal Ridge Vineyards. The sign also stated that visitors were welcome anytime.

"Anytime?" I asked.

"I've heard stories of people coming out here after everything is closed in town, but I've never done it. She has a small tasting room. I've heard she'll even make sandwiches for those who turn up hungry. She runs it almost like a small café."

"Is it important to have your own tasting room for visitors? Tom said they planned on having one."

"Yes, I think it is. It's one more way to attract people to your wine. A lot of people are drawn into the smaller vineyards by simply having a chance to taste some wines."

Sylvia maneuvered the Expedition off the driveway onto a dirt trail. It wouldn't qualify as a dirt road. We drove around a small house to a metal building that looked like it was used as a warehouse. A woman in dirty work boots, old jeans, and a Texas Tech sweatshirt approached us. She had thin, stringy grey hair that had definitely seen better days. She looked old and had one of those faces that looked like it had spent way too much time in the sun.

"Hi, Bee!" Sylvia shouted as she got out of the vehicle. "How are you doing today?"

"Got up on the right side of the ground today, so I got no complaints."

"This is Jim West, a friend of mine," Sylvia said.

"Hello, Bee," I said and extended my hand. She took it and surprised me with a grip that was a lot stronger than I would have imagined. Up close, she looked to be around eighty, stood a little bent over, and probably didn't weigh more than a hundred pounds.

"When you're done with this one, Syl, send him to me," she said. I knew she had to be joking, but I couldn't see it in her expression.

"We'll see. So far, he ain't been half bad," Sylvia said.

Her comment brought a chuckle out of the old woman. "Obviously, he's not from around here. Most of the pickin's here are a bit run down."

I didn't know what to say.

"That's true, Bee. Jim's from New Mexico."

"New Mexico?" she thought about it for a few seconds. "Been through there a few times. Hell, come on in and get the wine for the lady, young man. Let's see how strong you are."

I followed Bee and Sylvia into the small warehouse. Eight cases of wine were stacked up near the entrance. I took them one by one out to the Expedition, while the two women stood in the shade inside the building and talked. When I finished, they came out to the vehicle. Sylvia inspected how I'd packed the cases. Bee continued her inspection of me. Nobody made any comments, so I figured I passed their scrutiny.

We said our goodbyes and drove off.

"Isn't she a hoot?" Sylvia asked.

"Yes, she is," I said, although I wasn't quite sure what I thought of her.

"The next stop is another smaller vineyard not far from the Broken Spur," she announced.

"Smaller than hers? That didn't seem to be a very big operation."

"A little smaller," she said without any further clarification.

I figured I would see for myself.

"Did you know that this area, the Texas Hill Country Viticultural Areas, is the second largest viticultural area in the Unites States?"

"Maybe if I knew what viti-what-your-world meant," I said.

"From viticulture. Wine growing."

"Really? It's that big?"

"Yes," she said. "Texas has always been big into wine. Back around 1900, Texas already had a couple dozen wineries. Prohibition put a stop to their development, and only one of the original wineries reopened and managed to stay viable."

"Which one is that?"

"The Val Verde Winery down in the Del Rio area."

"But none of the ones around here or up in Lubbock?" I asked.

"No, but as you know a lot of new ones have flourished. Today Texas is one of the top five wine producing states in the country."

"I imagine California leads the nation."

"I think so, too" she said.

We got back on the highway and headed east again. Before long, we turned onto a dirt road winding our way through ranch land.

"That's part of the Rondit ranch over there," she pointed to our left.

"Don't know it."

"You know, Gary Rondit. He was at the open house."

"The skinny guy with short red hair," I said, more from a matter of elimination than remembering his name.

"Yes. His wife was the rather heavy one with the short curly grey hair," Sylvia said.

"Okay. I remember them. How large is his ranch?" I asked.

"I don't know, but it's big. I--"

Something hit the front windshield with a lot of force. Part of the windshield flew into the car and spider web cracks spread out from the center of the impact in less than a second. Sylvia screamed, and the Ford slid off the road, stopping on hard dirt. At first, I first thought a rock had hit us.

"Damn!" Sylvia cried out.

I looked over at her and saw her staring at her right hand. Blood was trickling out of a cut on her cheek where it looked like a shard of glass had cut her. She must have rubbed it with her hand, because now a small sliver of glass stuck out of her middle finger. Then I saw it.

"Duck down! Quick!" I shouted.

She ducked, at least as much as you can with a seat belt on. I realized then that we needed to move.

"No good," I said a little more calmly. "Drive us to behind those trees." A clump of small cedars, mountain laurels, and mesquite trees bunched up against the dirt road about fifty yards in front of us.

Her facial expression went from shock to comprehension. I

glanced out the window to our right. I could see forever, and the only thing out there was someone driving a tractor in the distance. She hit the gas and the Expedition shot forward onto the road and down a gentle slope to the only cover we had nearby. Sylvia braked hard and looked over at me.

"I don't think that was in the car when we left this morning." I pointed to a tear on the rear driver's side door panel, just above the window. More a gouge than a tear, she could easily see what I saw. A bullet, not a rock, had busted through the windshield. Luckily it had missed both of us, but it struck the door frame where it ripped through the vinyl and insulation, hit the medal frame, deflected toward the rear of the vehicle, and came to a rest after ripping through another two inches of the hard vinyl and softer insulation. The round was partially visible.

"Someone tried to shoot us?" she whispered.

"I didn't see anyone out there. A guy on a tractor, but I don't think he fired at us. I think it was just a random shot that wasn't directed at us. It just found us."

"What do we do?"

"I think we need to call 911, just to be sure," I said. "Two deaths in two days and now this."

"Think we have a serial killer out there?" Her face took on a wide eyed look of fear, and I thought she had started trembling.

I grabbed her cut hand. "Sylvia, look at me. We're okay now. You better get this glass out of your finger. I'll call the cops, but you'll need to explain to them where we are."

After we contacted the Sheriff's Office, I suggested Sylvia stay in the car while I looked around the area. I didn't see anything, so I hiked the fifty yards back to where we were when the bullet struck the car. I felt certain that the bullet striking the SUV was an accident. The only person in sight was the man on the tractor. It had to be three quarters of a mile away traveling in the same direction as before. Something didn't look right about the tractor, but at the same time, I didn't sense any threat from it. I returned to the Expedition somewhat surprised that Sylvia had stayed in the vehicle.

Deputy Stephens arrived first at the scene. His flashers were on, but he hadn't used his siren. He came alone.

"Now what's this about someone taking a shot at you?" he asked without any greeting.

"Hey, Deputy," I said in a friendly tone. He might not have remembered me, but I recognized him. "It may not be anything but an errant round, but it could have killed us."

"Were you at that scene the day before yesterday?" Recognition had finally settled in. Of course, he didn't have to specify the day. I'd been at a "scene" every day since my arrival.

"Yes, but I have no reason to suspect this has anything to do with that. This is Sylvia Scott."

Stephens turned to Sylvia and the two greeted each other.

"Did the bullet graze you?" he asked spotting the small cut on her face. It had already stopped bleeding, and Sylvia had cleaned her face and hand with something she must have had with her in the Ford.

"Glass," she said. "I'm fine, but look what happened to my Expedition." She led the deputy around the front of the vehicle and showed him the windshield.

"Sure it was a bullet?" he asked.

"Yes. Look in here," she said and opened the passenger side

front door. She pointed to the location, and Deputy Stephens peered in.

"Hell! The round is still there."

I felt like saying "Good eye, Sherlock," but wisely kept the sarcasm to myself. After all, Stephens seemed like a good guy.

We spent the next five minutes explaining why we were where we were when the round went through the windshield. Neither one of us saw anything. I did tell him about the man on the tractor, and that I didn't suspect him of the shooting.

A second county sheriff's sedan pulled up with two young deputies. Stephens immediately sent them to find and interview the man on the tractor. After they left, Stephens obtained Sylvia's permission to retrieve the round from her car. The two stood together talking by the open back driver's door. He first took a picture of the damage with the round still imbedded in the door frame. I heard him tell Sylvia to call him Jerry, and then a few seconds later say something like "You probably don't remember me."

She giggled in response to something else he said. I decided to walk away and let them flirt with each other in private. My lack of emotions surprised me. I tried not to be too introspective anymore, since I never knew if I had the right answers or not anyway. However, I did wonder why I felt no minute sense of jealousy. Sylvia and I had spent a lot of time together in the last forty eight hours. We had even slept together. I felt a growing attachment to her, but I didn't feel any right of ownership. In fact, for some unknown reason that I didn't understand, I hoped Deputy Stephens might be a good match for her.

I walked back up the slope to see if I could see the man on

the tractor and the other deputies, but they were all out of sight. Noise came from Deputy Stephens' sedan. The radio, I thought. I saw Stephens talking into his collar where his mobile microphone was attached. I couldn't hear his exact words, but something got him excited.

"Wait there!" he shouted at me. He jogged up the road. "Is this where the round struck the car?"

"Somewhere along here," I said. "The shot came from over there." I pointed across the field. The terrain wasn't flat, but we could see for at least a mile without any serious obstruction.

"Where was the tractor?"

"In the same line, right out there. It was moving to the right. What is that, west?"

"Close enough," he said. "Did you see anything beyond the tractor?"

"No. The person may have fired from the trees in the distance."

Stephens nodded and stared out across the horizon. I looked again, too, but still didn't see anything.

"What happened?" I finally asked him.

Sylvia had walked up to us.

"The guy driving the tractor is dead. Shot in the head."

Everything fell into place. We were never the target. The man in the tractor was. The person shooting at him had taken at least two shots. One hit the victim and the other hit us. Hell, he could've taken a dozen shots. The tractor noise would have drowned out the sounds of a weapon, most likely a rifle, fired from a distance. Bouncing along this dirt road with the windows up, we would never have heard anything either. About a mile of semi-flat terrain separated us from the trees.

"Did you say someone is dead?" Sylvia asked.

"Yes, the man operating the tractor," Stephens said.

"Oh, no. Do you know who it was?" she asked.

"Not at the moment."

"My God," she said softly.

"I'm sorry Sylvia, but I need to ask you to leave your Expedition here until our crime scene guys get out here."

"Why us?" she asked.

"Just to be thorough. They'll want to get the angle of impact, match it up with where you started your skid, and get the best probable location of the shooter. Your being here and getting hit is actually a break for us."

"But I have to pick up another batch of wine and get all this back," she said.

"Sorry, Sylvia. I really am, but we need to look at all this," Stephens said.

"He's right," I said. "Can't you get someone else to drive out here and help you finish up?"

"I guess so. How long will you need my car?" she asked.

"A couple of hours at most. We don't need to do anything to it. We'll take some photos and do some calculations, like I said. We'll also remove what's left of the bullet."

"Okay, Jerry, but I need my car back." She called someone on her cell phone. "He'll be here in a half hour." She didn't elaborate who he was, but I figured it was one of guys who worked for her.

Another sheriff's sedan approached us and two deputies jumped out of the car when it came to a stop. They both looked like they lifted weights. Their uniform shirts were stretched tight around their chests and biceps. They had short hair, but that's where the similarities stopped. One was over six foot and had a long face topped with blond hair. The other man looked a few years older, stood three or four inches shorter, had black hair, and sported what looked like a permanent five o'clock shadow on his face.

The three deputies huddled and discussed something. When they separated, Stephens left with the tall deputy, and the other deputy remained with us.

"I'll call you," Deputy Stephens called out the car window to Sylvia as they drove away.

"You know him?" I asked Sylvia.

"We've met before a couple times, but never when he was on duty. Actually, I was a little embarrassed that I didn't remember him."

The dark-haired deputy peered into the SUV.

"You two were lucky neither of you were hit by the bullet," he said after he closed the vehicle door.

"Yes, we were," I said. "What do you know about the man on the tractor who was shot?"

"Nothing yet. They had us come here first to spring Deputy Stephens. They wanted him free to go over there. He's got a lot more experience in these things than most of us. Where are you all going with all that wine?" He directed his question to me.

I looked over at Sylvia. Something about the way she looked made me think that this guy had already started to irritate her. She took a couple of breaths before answering.

"I own and operate Scott Distribution out of Fredericksburg. I pick up wine at a number of local vineyards and deliver them to a variety of customers in the area. The wine you refer to is some I picked up this morning."

"Oh, yeah, good, good," the deputy answered. "The crime scene guys should be here any minute. I think they're going to do your Expedition first."

"You're here protecting the evidence?" I asked.

"Yeah. Kind of have to do it."

Sylvia walked a few yards from us and stared off in the distance away from where the tractor had been. I sensed something wasn't right and walked over to her.

"You okay?" I asked.

"Yes," she said and reached out and grabbed my hand. "No, not really. I don't know what caused it. Maybe him, but all of a sudden I feel a need to scream or to hit something. I need to sit down."

Her face had become pale, and I thought she was about to faint. I helped her sit down on the dirt road, and I sat next to her.

"It's just all this excitement. It plays havoc with your adrenalin and nervous system. Believe me, I know this."

"You've been shot at before?" she asked.

"Hey, I'm an old hand at this. You'll be fine. The trick is to make the bullet miss. So far you're batting a thousand. The shakes will be gone before you know it." I rambled on. In a few minutes, she got her composure back.

"I thought I was going to faint," she said. "You don't really think they were shooting at us, do you?"

"No. The guy on the tractor was the target. We just got hit by a round that missed."

"You sure it wasn't the other way around?"

"Of course," I said, but for the first time I wondered about that possibility.

Chapter 7

Thirty minutes later, Sylvia's assistant, Trey, arrived. She and the wine left with him in his shiny white pickup truck. I stayed behind with a promise to bring the Expedition to her warehouse when the police had finished with it. She wanted to leave her assistant and have me continue on with her, but I convinced her that the police would need someone to answer questions and help them with placing the SUV where it was when the bullet struck the window.

Two crime scene specialists showed up five minutes after Sylvia left. They messed around inside the vehicle for a few minutes before asking me to drive it back to the exact spot where it had been. As Sylvia's reaction had been to drive the car off the road immediately after the impact, and I had already located where we went off the road, I had no trouble in placing the car very near to where it happened.

The two specialists debated the amount of deflection the window would have had on the round's trajectory. Finally, they agreed on the angle of impact and from that the probable location of the shooter. The same patch of trees that seemed obvious to me from the start. I knew the work had to be done, though. You can't tell the judge or the jury that anything is simply obvious.

When they released the Ford, I didn't drive directly back to town. I followed the two specialists as they drove to the other scene being worked. I saw the tractor tilted precariously downward into a roadside ditch. The driver was no longer on the tractor. I didn't know if he had fallen out or if he had been taken off the tractor. The body had already been enclosed in a body bag. Most of the dozen law enforcement and medical personnel stood around talking. It didn't seem like they could do much here.

The two crime scene guys grabbed Deputy Stephens and pointed in the direction where the shooting likely took place. I couldn't hear their conversation, but I saw him nod. In another second, the two specialists were joined by two other deputies and the four drove off. I assumed they went to help in the search for any evidence the shooter may have left behind.

Deputy Stephens saw me and waved me over.

"Why are you hanging around?" he asked.

"Curiosity, I guess."

"The guy's name is Wally Montrose. He's a farm hand, a ranch hand, did a lot of work for Bull Durham and occasionally for Mr. Rondit. Ever met him before?"

"No. Met the other two guys you mentioned at the Hasben's grand opening the other day, but never heard of him." I nodded toward the victim.

"No reason why you should," Stephens said. "We're thinking he was the intended target, not you two."

"I agree."

"When are you leaving town?"

"I was hoping tonight."

"Might not be a bad idea."

"What do you mean?" I asked.

"I don't know. Three guys killed, and there's a connection with each to you."

"Oh, come on, Deputy."

"Don't get me wrong, West. I don't think anyone thinks

you're involved." Of course that's what he would say even if he thought I was. "However, the killer, if it is one person, may wonder about you. He may not like having you as a possible, recurring witness."

"Not a very good witness since I don't know a damn thing about any of this," I said. "I wish I did. Why do you think this is connected with the other killings?"

"Just a hunch," he said. "We run about one homicide a year around here. Since your arrival, we've had three in as many days."

"I see why you might want me to leave town. Do you all have an idea what's going on?"

"We have some," he said. He didn't share.

"If they're linked, there has to be a connection."

"Thanks, Sherlock," he said.

I couldn't believe he stole one of my lines. No doubt I had worn out my welcome. Way too unfamiliar with the environment to piece anything together, I took my best course of action and left. Deputy Stephens' invitation for me to head home sounded good.

The Expedition had to get back to Sylvia's warehouse, but I couldn't resist driving around the area where the shooter had to have taken his shots. I knew the direction the deputies had driven when they left to go to the trees across the field. I drove off in the same direction and watched for a road or dirt trail that might lead me to the shooter's location.

After driving a half mile, I came to a dirt road that intersected the narrow paved road I was on. I took it to my left and before long saw the clump of trees and two parked sheriff's vehicles. As I approached the scene, a heavy set deputy in uniform stepped out onto the road and signaled me to stop and go away. Despite my curiosity, I stopped and started to back up. Looking around for a place to make a u-turn, I saw what looked like old wagon tracks to my right. They appeared to make a large, slow turn back in the direction I needed to go.

The dirt road had a small drop off on each side. It didn't look that severe, but I didn't want to get Sylvia's Expedition stuck out here. I studied the old wagon tracks and realized they were at least on flat ground. If they didn't go anywhere, I could easily make my u-turn and head to town. I drove the Ford off onto the tracks. They really did make me think of the tracks made by the old wagons and stage coaches after years of use.

The tracks slowly bent to my right, which I thought would be a good omen. However after driving just a couple hundred yards, the tracks bent back to the left and into another area of trees and thick underbrush. I stopped, and a man suddenly appeared in front of me. He carried a shotgun which he pointed at the ground in front of the Expedition.

He shouted at me to get out. I studied him for a second. Wally hadn't been shot with a shotgun, but I was trespassing. I showed him both my hands through the front windshield before I opened the door and stepped out of the Expedition.

He said something in a hand held radio or walkie-talkie, as we would have called it when I was a kid.

"Sorry if I'm trespassing. I was just trying to get back to the road," I said.

"Move away from the car!" he barked.

I took four or five steps to my left. He looked all business. He was black, looked to be in his mid-thirties, and kept a steady gaze on me.

"What are you doing out here?" he asked a little more calmly than his first command to me.

"I told you--"

"No! Why were you here in the first place?" His eyes started to bounce between me and the front windshield of the Expedition. I wondered if he recognized the damage as being caused by a bullet.

"There's been a shooting," I said.

"I know. You do it?"

"No. How about you?"

"If it was, I would've shot you by now," he said.

Not much of an argument, I thought, or even a real threat. The police were close now. They weren't even in the area earlier. I didn't peg him for the shooter, and some silly, macho piece of me wanted him to think he didn't scare me.

"The shooter didn't use a shotgun. One of his rounds struck the Expedition. One of the other ones killed a young man. I just left the police and thought I would come up here to see if they had developed any leads from the spot where the gunman fired at us. The cops up here didn't want to chat and told me to leave. It's not easy to do a u-turn on that dirt road over there," I motioned with my head toward the road. "I saw the tracks and thought I could use them."

He stared at me. I didn't know if he was thinking or waiting on whoever he talked to on the radio. "Where's the owner of that Expedition?" He still had the shotgun pointed at the ground in front of me.

"You know her?" I asked. "Give her a call and she'll tell you it's okay for me to be driving it. She can also verify everything I said." I didn't want to give him her name.

"Who do you have here?" a man asked behind me.

Surprised that I didn't hear his approach, I turned my head and saw Gary Rondit. While I knew I was on his property, I also recognized him as the red haired rancher I had met at the grand opening.

"I'm glad to see you," I said.

Before he said anything he walked around to the front of the Expedition and looked at the front windshield.

"It would be nice if your friend here stopped pointing his shotgun in my direction," I said.

"Yeah, Cappy, he's okay," Rondit said.

Cappy shouldered his shotgun but didn't look apologetic.

"You were trespassing," Cappy said to me. "You could've been a cattle rustler." He had the hint of a smile on his face.

"Jim, right? Jim West?" Rondit said.

"Yes. Have you talked to the police about the shooting this morning?"

"Terrible thing. Yes. Can't believe someone shot Montrose."

"Wally?" Cappy asked. "Is he okay?" He appeared to be truly concerned.

Rondit shook his head, and Cappy took a step backwards. I saw his hands tighten on the shotgun.

"Whoever shot him hit the Expedition with a round before they got him." My comment might not have been necessary, but I didn't want Cappy to focus any anger he had over Wally's murder toward me.

"What caliber rifle you think did that?" Rondit directed his question at Cappy.

Cappy looked at Rondit, and it seemed that the two acknowledged something that I didn't. Cappy walked over closer to the windshield.

"Can't be sure, but definitely a high powered rifle. Most likely a hunting rifle, maybe a thirty-ought-six. Missed you obviously." He directed this last comment toward me.

"Yes."

"Ms. Scott all right, too?" Rondit asked.

"Yes. A small piece of glass got her face and then her hand, but that's all. She had someone come out and help her finish her rounds, and I waited with the Expedition for the sheriff's men to finish with it."

"We thought we heard three shots earlier today," Rondit said. "They were spaced about fifteen seconds apart. Cappy and I were fixing a section of fence over east. At the time we thought someone might be hunting on a neighboring ranch. Didn't think much of it. Later we heard the sirens. About the same time I received a call from the sheriff's office. The woman deputy told me about the shooting on my property. Wouldn't tell me who at the time. Just got the name a few minutes ago. He was working for me today, you know." Rondit spit on the ground.

I didn't know it. "I hope they catch the guy," I said. A lame comment, but it came out of my mouth without much thought.

"We all do," Cappy said.

"Did you know him, Cappy?" I asked.

"Name's Hank, Hank Stewart," he said without offering a hand to shake. "Yeah, I knew him. Nice guy, a real nice guy. Can't believe anyone wanted to kill him. It must have been an accident; someone shooting at a rabbit or a bird, and the bullet just got him."

I didn't comment on my thoughts, but I was curious why

Rondit called him Cappy if his name was Hank Stewart.

"Well, West, these tracks don't go much further. You might as well make a u-turn and get back on the dirt road. Take that one to the paved road, and you should be able to find your way out of here." Rondit used his arms and hands indicating each turn I would take.

"Yeah, I think I'd better. Sorry about the trespassing. I guess after being shot at, I just let my curiosity get the better of me."

"Don't sweat it. Cappy and I haven't shot a trespasser in quite some while." Rondit grinned when he said it, but this was south central Texas.

I knew I needed to get Sylvia's Expedition back to her warehouse, so I headed there. My cell phone rang on my way back.

"Jim, I heard someone took a shot at you. Are you okay?" Tom Hasben asked.

"How did you already hear about that?"

"I ran into Sylvia at the Diamond. She told me all about it. I just left her. I think she's still shaken up."

"Well, that's the normal reaction. As she probably told you, the bullet missed both of us but did some damage to her Expedition," I said.

"She said someone else was killed. Who was it? Do you know?"

"No one I knew." Even though I knew the name, I wanted to let the police notify next of kin before the rumor mill spread it around town like wildfire.

"I can't believe this is happening here. It's like we're back in D.C."

"Hopefully, the cops will catch whoever's doing this soon."

"Jim, can we get together for lunch? I need to talk to you for a minute."

"Can we do it over the phone?" I asked.

"I'd rather not."

I agreed, and he suggested a Mexican restaurant in Fredericksburg. Despite my friendship with Tom, I really had better things to do with my time.

When I finally found the Scott Distribution warehouse, I learned that Sylvia had not yet returned. The young woman handling the phones said that Sylvia had called and left a message for me. She handed me a note that she must have written after talking to Sylvia on the phone. She could have read it to me. The note was folded in half and my name was written on the outside. Maybe she thought she was somehow honoring my privacy.

The message requested that I please stop by later in the afternoon since she had been detoured into some other business. She said she would wait for me if I came late, but that she really wanted to see me before I left for home.

I figured I'd give her until five. My lunch with Tom would last an hour or two. I could kill a couple of hours, but then I needed to head home if I was to get there before midnight.

Lunch with Tom did last nearly two hours. It took him the first twenty minutes and two top shelf margaritas before his agitation simmered down. Somehow, he had discovered the identity of the latest victim. The murder of the farmhand Wally Montrose had shaken him. Wally had helped him out on a couple occasions. He liked Wally and thought everyone else in the Hill Country did too. He mentioned that Wally had gotten serious about some girl recently. He and Wally even had a hypothetical discussion about using the Broken Spur as a wedding venue.

Once he got past the shooting, he started ranting again about how Brenda was still overreacting to Lynn's text.

"I told Brenda that if she didn't stop dumping on me for something I didn't do, that maybe I should go ahead and do something with Lynn. At least then I would deserve all the harassment."

"I imagine that comment went over quite well," I said.

He admitted it hadn't. Finally we started talking about people we used to know and places we had been with the air force. We knew quite a few of the same people from our two assignments together. I fought off the temptation to ask him about the woman with the frizzy hair and bad teeth that Brenda had mentioned.

By the time we parted, he had calmed down quite a bit. I suggested he take some flowers home to Brenda. He said he would. I watched him drive off. Sylvia hadn't called, so I thought I'd take a walk through the downtown area.

Fredericksburg is a small city. The downtown is not extensive, but there are a number of interesting stores, bars, and restaurants. Besides the exercise, the walk could be entertaining for a while. I hadn't gone far when someone called my name.

I turned around and saw trouble herself, Lynn the realtor and home wrecker.

"Jim? Right? That's you," she said.

"Yes, and you're Lynn."

"You remember. That's sweet. Didn't you just feel awful for poor Tom? His opening was a disaster."

"Yes, and for Brenda, too," I said.

"Oh, of course." I thought she said the "of course" a little too insincerely. "Did you ever find that property you were looking for?"

"I didn't have anything specific in mind."

"I'd be happy to show you around," she said.

"Thanks, but I'll be heading back to New Mexico later today."

"It's getting late for a drive that long. Why don't you let me buy you a drink? Stick around for a while longer."

Had I lost total control of the situation? I wondered. Too many things tugged at me in too many directions. Despite my realization that the overwhelming winner in my internal, mental debate was to say no to Lynn and move on, I ended up following her into a nearby pub. I could claim that my attraction to beer was the reason I followed her, but I knew somewhere in the back of my mind lingered the image of her in the video.

She wore a dark blue dress that clung to her and dark heels that looked too dangerous to walk in. We sat at a small table close to the bar and ordered a couple draft beers. I realized when she sat down that the front of her dress was cut low. It would take an effort to maintain eye contact.

"So what do you think of our little town?"

"I like it here. There's a lot more to do around here than I realized. Have you always lived here in the area?" I asked.

"No, my family moved down here from Dallas when I was seven. I guess that almost makes me a native."

"Ever have the urge to move back to the big city?"

"All the time," she said. "I think I will at some point, but what's that saying?"

She paused either to try to remember the saying herself or to wait for me to tell her. However, I had no idea what saying she had in mind.

"You know. Better to be a big fish in a small pond, than just another small fish in a big pond."

I wondered if she meant the real estate business or something else.

"It's hard to walk away from something that's working," she said.

"That's true."

"I heard through the grapevine that you've been working with the police on these recent killings. What's going on?"

"I've been involved, but only because I've been at the wrong place at the wrong time." I figured I could throw out a few old sayings myself.

"But surely the police have confided in you."

"No," I said.

"Well, the word's going around town that you're some kind of secret agent and that all this is related to you."

The Internet had improved the efficiency of small town gossip, if not the accuracy. Unfortunately, I had made the news more than I would have liked in the last few years.

"How about you? What do you know about the shootings?" I decided to try to direct the conversation away from me.

"Nothing. Nothing at all. In fact, it frightens me. I'm out a lot at night, and this stuff scares me. Someone is being killed every day. Makes me afraid to go out at night."

"That's understandable. It is scary. Somebody shot a hole in Sylvia's Expedition today."

"What? I hadn't heard that. You say Sylvia Scott's SUV?"

"Yes."

Her mind worked for a few seconds. "I heard that maybe you and Sylvia have hit it off already?"

"Hit it off?" I guess she had more interest in learning about whatever relationship Sylvia and I had developed than the fact that someone had shot a hole in Sylvia's windshield while we were in the vehicle.

"Oh, you know what I mean." Her focus turned to the pub's main entrance. The expression on her face changed. She looked pleased about something. "Look who's here."

I saw a white haired man, about sixty-five years old, walk in to the pub. Something about him, maybe his clothes, his boots, or the silver belt buckle the size of a dinner plate gave me the idea he had money. He stood straight and tall.

"Jim, dear, he's an old friend. I must go say hello. You will excuse me." She got up, took her drink, and went over to the man.

They hugged and sat at a table at the door. She immediately grabbed his hand and more than once rubbed his arm. It only took me ten minutes to realize she wasn't coming back. I had the mixed feelings of relief and of being ditched.

As I walked by them, she at least gave me a furtive smile and waved a couple fingers. She had apparently latched onto bigger prey. Outside, I noticed a city police vehicle parked across the street. The two men inside looked away when I saw them. Had to be nothing, I told myself. I hadn't done anything to warrant police surveillance.

Storm clouds were building in the west. The wind had also picked up, putting a touch of a chill in the air. I saw the coffee shop down the street. The sight of it made me curious about the young man who was shot. I didn't remember his name. I walked to the coffee shop, and just before going inside, I looked back for the police sedan. It had disappeared.

A half dozen vases filled with an assortment of flowers adorned various spots inside the coffee shop. Cards had been taped to the vases. I glanced at one and realized the flowers had been gifts to the coffee shop by the local community expressing sympathy and support. More vases occupied the place than customers. I wondered if that was due to people's reluctance to go to a location where a crime had recently occurred. Not unlike the reluctance of those searching for a new home to buy a house where a murder had just taken place.

The same cashier, the one who took my order on the day of the shooting, worked the counter. She didn't recognize me at first, but after she ran my order through the register, she glanced curiously at me.

"How are you all doing?" I asked.

"Okay. You were here that day?" She said it as half question and half statement.

"Yes. How's the man who got shot doing?"

"Cisco's going to be okay," she said with a big smile. "He won't be able to come back to work for a long while, but we've been told after a few months he should be just like normal."

"Great."

I sat at a table by the window and looked out at the busy street. I hadn't told the cashier that the healing process didn't end with the physical recovery. There would be mental and emotional trauma that also needed healing. For many, healing comes with time, but for some it has lifelong effects.

"Here's your cappuccino," said the cashier as she sat down my drink.

"Oh, I could've come and gotten it."

"Did you hear that the girl who was taken from here was found dead?" she asked.

"Yes. So was the guy who took her away. Both are dead now."

"That's really scary. I didn't hear about the guy, but I'm glad he's dead. We were all afraid he might come back. We saw him, you know."

I nodded.

"Two girls quit. They were afraid he would come back to get rid of the witnesses."

"He won't be coming back now," I said.

"Good. Do you know why he kidnapped her?" she asked.

"No, I don't. I don't think the police do either."

"Someone said they heard that she had been forced to marry the guy and that she was trying to get away."

"Forced to marry him? By whom?" I asked.

"I don't know. It's just something that someone said. Maybe a cult or something like that."

"Are there any cults around here?"

"Not that I know of. There was that Branch Davidian one that wasn't too far from here. You know, they made girls as young as ten marry these old creeps. Can you imagine that?" she asked.

"No, I can't."

"It happened, you know."

"Oh, I believe you. I heard about it, too. I'm just saying that I can't imagine why people are like that." I actually could imagine it. I had been involved in too many pedophile investigations not to. If I were ever made king of the world, people might be surprised how far I would expand the death penalty.

After she went back to the counter, I wondered about the cult possibility. That would be something the police should easily be able to follow up, if they haven't already. If she was running from a bad marriage, why would she still be wearing the wedding ring? I wondered if she still had the ring on when the police found her body. I remembered then that someone had mentioned to me she wasn't married, that the ring had been her mother's.

I called my neighbors for the second time in two days. Their kids took care of my dog Chubbs whenever I was gone from home. I told them that I was stuck in Fredericksburg longer than I thought I would be. They said it was no problem. I knew their kids didn't mind. They got along great with Chubbs and made more money with my delay.

A local newspaper occupied a vacant table nearby. I grabbed it and glanced through it to see what the latest might be on the killings. I found a short article on page three that said the police were pursuing leads. The article identified the first victim, Frances Wilikin, but said that the second victim had still not been identified. Nothing new, I thought, but I wondered if the police knew more by now.

Sylvia finally called. She made it back to her warehouse and asked if I would come over. I told her I would. The approaching storm clouds looked ominous. I wondered if I would make it to her warehouse before it started raining. If the hotel was any closer, I would've gone there first to retrieve my car. I walked towards Sylvia's place. No cop cars appeared to be following me. I didn't expect any, but the one I spotted earlier had put a few paranoid doubts in my mind.

The sky darkened. The sidewalk crowds thinned out as the sound of thunder reached the city. I kept walking. Although I prepared myself to jump into the nearest open establishment if the rain came, I reached the Scott Distribution Company office and warehouse before the rain.

Sylvia surprised me with a hug and a kiss as soon as I walked in.

"I don't know what I would've done today if you hadn't been there!"

"You did okay. You would have done just fine without me," I said. "How did the rest of the day go?"

"Long. In addition to my stop, Hank had an appointment to help one of our suppliers with a bottling issue. We made a lot of points, but I mostly sat around and watched them work."

"Hank? You know there's another guy around here named Hank."

She looked at me curiously.

"Hank Stewart, a black guy."

"Oh yes, nice guy, I know him," Sylvia said.

A loud boom of thunder shook the building.

"I think this storm may hit us," I said.

"You should be a weatherman," she said grinning. "I've already sent everyone home to beat the storm. It's quitting time anyway, but they usually stay until I either leave or chase them out of here. It's a good crew."

"Can I do anything for you to help out?"

"You've done a lot already today. Did they say who the guy

was who was shot?"

"Name was Wally Montrose, or something like that."

"Wally? Oh no, that's too bad," she said with some emotion.

"You know him?"

"Not well, but I met him on a couple of occasions. He's a," she paused, "was a good guy. Nice, quiet, and from what I was told, hard working. I remember him always being very polite. Why would anyone want to kill him?"

"Sounds like what both Deputy Stephens and Tom Hasben said about him," I said.

"He worked odd jobs for a few of the ranchers. Why would anyone want to kill him?"

"I don't know." I figured she repeated the question out of disbelief, rather than any expectation that I would have the answer.

"It's easier for me to imagine they were shooting at us," she said.

"Now that's not a good thought."

Her office phone rang. I walked around the small office looking at the pictures on the walls while she talked to a customer on the phone.

"That was the manager from the Goat. It's a new place in town trying to survive. He wanted to know if I might be able to give him anything new to try. What he means is he's looking for free samples."

"They do that?"

"Of course. I don't blame them. It's a very hard world out there, Jim."

"I know."

"This gives me a great chance to give him some Broken Spur

wine. Tom and Brenda gave me some bottles to use as free samples. They need people to try it as much as the Goat needs free stuff to sell. It's advertising, marketing, begging, call it what you will, but for new businesses, it's commonplace."

"Do we need to take it to them?" I asked.

"No way. He can pay for the gas. He's coming right over. Apparently they have a group in celebrating something and they've run low."

A few large raindrops hit the window. Sylvia started to put on a light jacket.

"I'll get the wine. Where is it?" I said.

"Do you mind? It's just inside the door to your right. The cases are stacked against the wall. Bring the cab."

"A whole case?" I asked.

"Yes. I won't give him the whole case, but I haven't decided how much I'll give him yet."

"Be right back," I said.

I jogged the twenty yards from her small office to the warehouse. The rain still hadn't started falling in earnest. I opened the metal door and looked for a light switch. I didn't see one, but decided there was just enough light in the building to find the wine. I located the cases and was looking for the cabernet sauvignon when I heard a noise that came from the back of the building.

Chapter 8

It could've been anything. I stood still listening for another sound. Sylvia had said she sent all her employees home. I hoped I wasn't getting paranoid. However, a few hours ago a bullet almost hit me, so maybe a little paranoia was prudent at the moment.

Two choices faced me. I could simply walk out. If I mentioned the sound to Sylvia, she would want to investigate. I would be right back here with her. That could put her at risk and complicate things for me. I decided to check out the sound without her and began to walk as quietly as I could around the shelving toward the back of the warehouse. The building wasn't very large. As far as warehouses go, it would be considered small. Yet it contained enough junk, along with rows of shelving, and stacks of wine cases to make hiding a cinch.

I heard another faint sound that could've been the creaking of a shoe or something slightly crunchy being stepped on. Almost a minute passed by while I waited to hear something else. An idea popped up into my mind that I should call out a warning. If I let the intruder know that I was aware of him, he would likely flee. That might have been the safest thing to do, but I didn't do it. I took a few more steps toward the back of the building.

In fact, I thought I was doing a pretty good job of sneaking up on whoever might be there. The sound of something falling to the cement floor behind me tricked me into looking back. It registered in my mind as the oldest trick in the books at about the same time I sensed something coming fast at the side of my head.

I ducked and a bottle of wine glanced off my skull. It hurt but did no damage. Off balance, I couldn't do much to fend off my attacker, who was already swinging the bottle down at my head again. I managed to deflect the bottle enough with my hand, so it struck the top of my left shoulder. The blow forced me unceremoniously into a sitting position in front of my attacker. He gave up on the still intact bottle of wine and kicked out at me with a boot.

I rolled to my right, and his boot grazed my side. Unfortunately, my roll pressed me up against some shelving. He had me trapped. My only way out was through him, and he had somehow found a crowbar. He held the crowbar above his head in his right hand and had transferred the wine bottle to his left. I hadn't suffered any real injury, but if he started hitting me with that crowbar my status could change quickly.

I could tell something in his mind cautioned him against using the crowbar. He had come in here to pinch a few bottles of wine, and now he could end up killing someone. We stared at each other for a few seconds.

Boom! The sound exploded close to us. We both cringed. I knew the sound hadn't come from thunder.

"On the ground!"

I looked over and saw Sylvia. She had a shotgun aimed at my attacker. Dust, debris, and a few drops of water were falling from a new hole in the warehouse's roof high above her head. By the time I looked back at my assailant, he was already on the ground. He still had the crowbar in one hand and the bottle of wine in the other. Both hands were stretched out in front of him.

I got to my feet, brushed the dust off my clothes, and wondered why I felt more embarrassed than injured.

"Are you okay, Jim?" she asked.

"Yes. I would've had him under control in a few more seconds myself," I said in jest.

"It looked like he was about to surrender," she grinned. "If you have your phone, will you dial 911 for me?"

"Please, ma'am. I'll put everything back," the man on the ground said while I dialed. "Don't call the police. I'll do whatever you want."

"Shut up," she said. "I could still shoot you, and you know the authorities wouldn't care a bit."

I didn't think she was correct, but I kept my thoughts to myself.

"Do you think he might have been the one who took a shot at us?" she whispered to me.

"I think he's just a petty thief trying to score some free wine."

"Yeah, maybe so. Someone did break-in and steal four cases of wine from this building a month ago."

"Sylvia? You in there?" a man shouted from the front entrance.

"One minute," she shouted back. "Jim, think you could watch him for a few minutes?" She held the shotgun out to me before I answered.

I took it, and she hurried off to meet her customer. She had only been gone a few seconds, when I heard police sirens.

"Damn!" the man on the ground said.

He looked like he was in his early twenties, maybe an inch taller than me, and twenty pounds lighter. I should have been able to handle him, I thought, but he had me off balance our entire short scuffle.

"You know I wasn't going to hit you with the crowbar," he said.

"Sure," I said, although I had wondered about that at the time.

"Crap, I didn't need it. I could've kicked your ass without it, old man."

"Well, we'll never know now, will we?" I said. "Were you the guy that broke in here before and stole some of the lady's wine?"

He ignored my question and mumbled something else about how tough he was. I couldn't quite understand him and didn't care to ask him to clarify. I decided long ago that fighting wasn't something I enjoyed.

"In here," I heard Sylvia call out from the front of the warehouse. A few seconds later, Sylvia led two police officers through the warehouse to the two of us. I recognized the woman officer immediately. I didn't know the young man with her.

"Mr. West, why doesn't it surprise me that you're involved in this?" Officer Morris said. "Three murders and a burglary in three days in our otherwise peaceful town, and you're present for all of them. Maybe I should've had dinner with you."

Sylvia gave me an inquisitive look.

"By the way, would you mind putting that shotgun away? You're safe now. We're here." Morris said.

I handed the shotgun to Sylvia. She walked back toward the front of the warehouse with it.

"Jimmy, cuff the guy and take that crowbar for evidence,"

Morris said. She didn't appear to be interested in the bottle of wine. "I understand this guy was beating the crap out of you until Sylvia rescued you." I started to say something, but she continued talking. "Want to tell me how this all happened."

"I was kicking his ass," the idiot on the ground claimed.

"Jimmy, see if the tough guy has any ID and check him for other weapons. Now, West, want to tell me how all this happened?" she repeated.

The two of us walked a few paces away, and I explained how I had come into the warehouse to retrieve some wine for Sylvia. When I finished talking, she nodded, and walked back to the burglar, who was now sitting up. She motioned to Jimmy, and the two strolled off to where she and I had been a few seconds earlier. While she and Jimmy talked, Morris kept her eyes on her prisoner.

"You didn't even hurt me," I said to the prisoner.

"You fight like my sister," he replied.

"Hey, no talking to the prisoner," Officer Morris instructed. "Your name is Mike, right?" she asked him.

"Yes."

"Well, we're going to give you a ride down to headquarters, Mike," she said. "If you have a car here, Jimmy can drive it down there for you. That way if you get out tonight, you'll have your wheels with you. You want him to do that?"

"I guess so," he said.

The poor guy was an idiot, I thought. He just gave the police permission to enter his vehicle.

"West, I need you to follow us down to give us a formal statement and swear out a complaint to go along with the break-in. It won't take long."

I wondered how much of Morris' comments were intended for Mike to hear rather than for me. Adding the assault charge had to get his attention and make him start thinking about the extent of trouble he found himself.

"I hadn't taken anything yet," the prisoner volunteered. "The back door was wide open."

Morris walked the half dozen steps to the back door. "I wonder if the crowbar will match the damage done on this door," she said.

This time Mike kept his mouth shut. His look on his face had turned defiant. Had he finally realized no one intended on cutting him any deals tonight? They took him out handcuffed and looking defeated. I didn't feel the least bit sorry for him. I never understood why guys like him went the route of burglary and crime rather than simply get a job.

Before they left, the police asked Sylvia to do an inventory to see if anything was missing. She didn't look thrilled at the prospect of more work.

"Just how strong are these bottles?" I asked. "That guy hit me twice with this one, and I don't think it did anything to the bottle."

"They do break, I assure you. Your head was just too mushy to break it."

"It was only a glancing blow. He hit my shoulder pretty hard with it though. Can I buy this one from you?" I asked.

"You saved it from being stolen, along with who knows how many more bottles. Take it as your reward."

"When I get done with the police want me to come back?"

"That would be great, except my mom's on her way over right now. She's already insisting that she stay with me or I stay at her place tonight," she said.

"That's nice."

"I think she wants to grill me about you as much as ensure my safety."

"Me?"

I didn't get an answer. It dawned on me that I didn't have my car. I should've asked one of the cops for a lift. Sylvia ended up giving me a lift to the station. I reminded her about her mother coming, but she thought she would be back before her mom's arrival. She sent her mother a quick text before we drove off. When she left me at police headquarters, she gave me a little wave and a look that I could've interpreted many ways.

I had my souvenir bottle of wine with which my assailant tried to crush my head.

Inside the police station, Jimmy had been replaced by the equally young Officer Creighton.

"You remember Officer Creighton from the other night?" Officer Morris asked.

"Of course."

"He's going to take your statement. I need to brief the boss and check on a few things. Creighton, make sure he tells you how Ms. Scott saved his ass tonight. I'll be back before long," She laughed softly to herself as she walked away.

Creighton was efficient and polite. We finished before Morris returned. I tried to leave, but he insisted I hang around until Morris showed up. My delay lasted only five minutes.

"How about that dinner?" she asked.

I didn't know how to politely say no. "Sure," I said.

"There's a great place around the corner. It's cheap, don't worry," she said.

"Am I buying?" I asked as we walked out.

"I don't think it would be ethical if I did. It might be perceived as my trying to bribe a witness."

She took me to what many might think of as a dive. The restaurant consisted of a small, rundown, wooden building that smelled of smoke as soon as we got near it. The good kind of smoke – barbeque. Inside, customers packed the place. We managed to find a table that hadn't been cleaned in a far corner. Morris called to an old man who was wiping a spill up off the floor nearby. He hurried over, said hello to Morris, and wiped off our table with the same cloth he had been using on the floor.

"He's a great guy," she said after he left.

"Did he call you Cat?" I asked.

"Yes. It's been my nickname ever since I was a kid."

"After the cat in the TV commercials?"

"Yes. Good guess. I'm used to it. I don't think half the people who know me even know my real first name," she said.

"Which is?"

"Carolyn."

"Not too far from Cat," I said.

Based on her suggestion, we each ordered a platter of brisket and ribs. It came with onion rings and a pitcher of beer. I was in heaven. We talked before our dinner came, but once it was there, our focus turned to the food. Other than the occasional comment that something was delicious, we didn't talk until the last bite had been swallowed. A pile of paper towels covered with grease and barbeque sauce sat next to each of our plates.

"How do you like police work?" I asked when the last piece of meat had been chewed off the last rib.

"I like it. Went to college down in San Marcos for a couple

of years. When my dad passed on, I came back to help my mother. Waitressed for a while, but we needed more money than I could earn doing that. I tried being a secretary, but that was no fun at all. Later, I went to school to be a dental hygienist. That didn't last a semester. God, I couldn't stand looking into some of the mouths I saw. I saw an ad to come work for the police department. Been happy ever since."

"Good for you. I enjoyed my time in law enforcement."

"I understand you were a military special agent but not military police."

"That's right."

"What's the difference?" she asked.

"The military police performed security for the installation, took care of traffic, handled misdemeanors, and responded to emergency calls. They performed an important function, but the investigations of felony offenses were handled by the OSI. NCIS did it for the navy and CID for the army."

She nodded as though she understood what I said. "How long did you do it?"

"Twenty years, then I retired and moved west."

"New Mexico, right?"

"Yes," I said. "Clovis, up by Amarillo and Lubbock."

"Guess you aren't going back tonight," she said.

I shook my head.

"What's your take on all this killing that followed you into town?"

"It doesn't have anything to do with me," I said. I started getting a little defensive until I realized she was teasing me again. "How come you keep picking on me?"

"Oh, come on. You're an easy target. Really, what do you

think is going on?

"I don't know. I would guess that the second victim got killed by someone who blamed him for killing the first girl."

"Frances Wilikin," she said.

"Yeah. Did you ever ID that guy?"

"Not yet, and that's slowing everything up. No hit with his prints. No one recognized him. We're working his DNA, but that'll take forever. We don't have any of the weapons used. Today we get the third victim, and we have no idea why anyone would want to kill him. It would make more sense to us that someone was actually shooting at you."

"No," I said. "I've been thinking about that. The tractor was between the trees and us when the shot hit the Expedition. He was okay when I first saw him. Later when I looked at him, he had moved on. That was when I thought something wasn't right. I realize now that he was slumped over."

"So if the guy shot from the trees where we think he did, the shot that hit the car came before the shot that hit the victim. Makes sense. Remind me tomorrow to tell the Lieutenant about that."

"Am I going to see you tomorrow?" I asked.

"If you're lucky."

The server showed up with two frosted mugs of beer. We had finished the pitcher, and I didn't know we had ordered any more beer.

"I didn't know if you could finish off your half of another pitcher," Cat said.

"What do you use, hand signals?" I asked more interested in how the server knew to bring the mugs of beer than responding to her verbal jab at my ability to drink my share of a pitcher of beer.

She ignored my question.

"One more thing you might want to look into, Cat. I hear Wally had talked about marrying some girl. She might know something about why anyone would want to kill him."

"I wonder if she's a good shot. By the way, how serious are you and Sylvia?"

"I only met her a few days ago," I said.

"Does that mean something?"

She had me there, but the problem was that I didn't know myself. "I really like her, but she knows I'm leaving soon. Like tomorrow, if possible, and I may not be back. That's not much of a foundation for a relationship."

"Two ships passing in the night?"

I didn't have a response. Our conversation paused.

"Oh, don't look at me like that. For your information, I make it a habit not to take possible murder suspects home to bed," she said.

I liked Cat, more than I would've expected, but I didn't have any desire to spend the night with her either. I certainly hadn't looked at her in any suggestive manner. "No steady man in your life?"

"In between steady men, if there really is such a thing as a steady man."

We talked and sipped our beer a while longer. Our discussion focused on life in Fredericksburg again. She appeared to be content with her life here. I even noticed some pride in her voice when she discussed Texas, the Hill Country, and Fredericksburg.

"It's really a friendly town," she said. "Did you know that

the first letter of the street names leading east and west along Main Street spell out 'ALL WELCOME'? Further along they spell 'COME BACK."

"No, I didn't know that. It's a nice touch. You ought to be a travel guide in your spare time," I said.

"I do some volunteer work with the schools. It's fun."

A little while later, we emptied our glasses and called it a night. She went back to the station. It took me a second to remember that I hadn't driven my car to the police station or the restaurant. It took almost an hour to walk to the hotel and my car. Luckily, the storm had passed and the weather remained pleasant, and the hotel had a vacancy. I checked back in for the night. I got a different room, but as they all looked alike, it didn't really matter.

I fell asleep vowing to myself to stay in bed until noon.

Chapter 9

The knock on my hotel room door came a lot earlier than I would've liked. I had already shoved aside my internal alarm clock, believing a day in bed would be safer for me than venturing outside. I had given up on ever seeing my home again.

I slipped into my dirty jeans and opened the door.

"Good morning, West. We got some breaks last night, and I want you to go along on a ride with me." Lieutenant Martin looked impatient standing in the hall.

"Only if it will get me out of this town any faster," I said.

"Get dressed. You don't need to shave. I'll be downstairs. Don't take long."

"You should've been a drill sergeant," I said. He went downstairs, and I joined him five minutes later.

"Grab a cup of coffee. We're going for a ride," he said.

A few seconds later, we were speeding out of town. "What's going on, Lieutenant?"

"We're helping the Sheriff out, and you're my ticket to the show."

"I think I'm still missing something."

"You made a remark last night that put us onto a new angle in these killings."

"I did?" I asked.

"You mentioned to Morris that Wally, the third victim, had a fiancée."

"Don't tell me she shot him." I remembered that's what Cat had speculated.

"No, wrong angle. Frances Wilikin was his fiancée."

"You're kidding," I said.

Martin shook his head. "Talked to his momma late last night. She was aware of the young girl's murder, but never paid close enough attention to get the girl's name from the news. She only had the two boys. She's taking Wally's death hard."

"Understandable, but what's all this got to do with me?"

"Apparently, Wally had been worried about the situation that Frances had gotten into at this communal ranch down south of here."

I still didn't know why I was tagging along. We were on a back road, and Martin was driving too fast around the corners.

"Do you really need to drive this fast?" I asked.

He slowed down. "Deputy Stephens and I talked this morning. The Sheriff doesn't see a need for the city's involvement, but Stephens convinced him it wouldn't hurt to have you there just to look at everyone to see if a face pops out." He saw the doubtful look I gave him. "Hey, I know it's a long shot, but it gets me there, and that's important to me."

"I wonder why Wally didn't mention the girl's death to his mother?"

"Good question, but we came up with a lot of possibilities this morning," he said.

"How early do you all start your day?" I asked. It did seem he had accomplished a lot before seven.

He ignored my question. "Wally may not have even known about her death until hours after the body was discovered. He lived alone in a small apartment near town. It may have been longer before he heard it on the news, and then he's dead within forty-eight hours of her murder."

I thought his math might be off a little. "Still, you'd think he would tell his mother. How about his father?"

"A truck driver. He's heading back here. He was in Nebraska when the shooting occurred."

"Any possibility Wally killed our second victim?" I asked.

"Our second victim? You on the payroll now?" he asked grinning.

"I should be."

"Yeah, I think Wally could've killed the guy. I would've."

I thought I might have, too, if I were in Wally's shoes. "If that's the case, it makes you wonder who killed Wally. Put them all in gangs, and it would sound like the beginning of a gang war."

"Thankfully, the gangs we have around here don't amount to much. More wanna-be gangs than the real things you find in the big cities. Besides, Wally is, I mean was, the farthest thing from the gang type."

"Have you learned anything significant from any of the crime scenes?" I asked. I didn't expect him to tell me, but he did drag me out of bed this morning.

Martin looked over at me for a second. I could tell he was trying to decide how much he should say.

"We've learned enough to know that nothing fits. We're even starting to have doubts whether our first male victim killed the girl." He paused for a second, but I didn't say anything hoping that he would continue. He did. "The girl may have been sexually assaulted just before she was killed. Blood type of her assailant didn't match our second victim. DNA will take a while longer."

"That only tells you that some other guy sexually assaulted her. Doesn't tell you who sliced her throat open," I said.

"I know, but it confuses everything. It brings in a second, totally unknown suspect."

"I suppose you're checking the blood type from whatever evidence you have with Wally's blood type."

"That would be a surprising match, but it didn't match his," he said. "We do know that Wally owned a revolver. Same caliber as the slug that killed the first male victim, but we haven't located it."

"That fits," I said. "He knew about her problems with the guy. When he heard about her kidnapping and death, he went after the guy. He might not have intended to kill him."

"Shooting a guy in the side of the head at close range usually means the shooter had intent."

"I meant when he first went after him, he may not have planned on killing him. By the way, did you find the round that killed the guy?" I asked.

"Wally or the other guy?"

"The other guy."

"No, but we're pretty good at telling the caliber from the entrance wound," he said.

Good, but not exact, I thought. I had to admit to myself that I had the bug to find out what was behind all this. I also still felt a debt to Frances Wilikin. I figured that debt had been partially erased by the kidnapper's own death. However, I now knew that a second man might have been involved in her death.

"You think the second victim was killed where the body was found?"

"No, but we're working a few angles on that."

We turned onto a driveway that shot in a straight line about a half mile to a large house.

"This is it," he said.

"What exactly do you want me to do?" I asked.

"Stick close to me. Keep your eyes open and your mouth shut. When we get done, let me know if you remember seeing anyone before."

Two sheriff's sedans were parked near the house. Martin parked his unmarked car next to them. Deputy Stephens must have been looking for us. He walked out of the house when we arrived.

"We may have hit the gold mine here, Marty," Stephens said after we all shook hands. "Wilikin lived here as a volunteer employee. Your guy did some odd jobs here, too. His name is Benjamin Lunce."

"Super," Martin said. "What do they know about the killings?"

"Allegedly nothing, but I think once we separate them all we may learn more."

"What's the plan?" Martin asked.

"Come on in and talk to them about your victim. I just got his name out of them. I didn't press for more. I figured I'd listen to what they tell you and see if anything new or any discrepancies pop out. Deputies Cooper and Samson are here, too. They know you have your end of the investigation to pursue. They won't give you any grief."

I already knew there was conflict between the Sheriff's Office and the Fredericksburg PD. For one thing, the two agencies almost lived together in the city with their respective offices located side by side. Even their substations were within a city block of each other. Such bad blood isn't unusual and is usually due to individual egos. I decided to stay neutral. I didn't anticipate recognizing anyone, but I would listen and learn like Martin and Stephens.

In a large room that might have been considered the house's great room, an elderly couple and six college age kids sat on overstuffed furniture. The older couple, Simon and Bell Miller, owned the property and operated it as a communal ranch. The six young adults received free room and board for working the ranch. They had no obligation to stay, but if they wanted to stay and eat, they had to work. Four of the six were taking a break from college, and two had separately discovered the ranch while drifting around trying to find themselves. At least, that's what they all claimed.

There were four young men and two women. I pegged them all to be within a year or two of one side of twenty or the other. One of the college guys appeared to be attached to the girl taking a break from college. He kept touching her arm as they answered questions, and once she reached for his hand. I didn't see any sign that the other four were anything but acquaintances.

Over the past fifteen years, or ever since Simon and Bell started accepting volunteer help, dozens of young men and women had helped out at the ranch. The couple only ever wanted to know the volunteers' names, which they acknowledged could have easily been made up. They did have hundreds of pictures of the volunteers and still stayed in touch with a lot of them. Some stayed for a few weeks, others stayed longer. They could remember only two volunteers having stayed for over a year.

Frances arrived in May and planned to leave next month, November, to marry Wally. Something happened recently that had frightened her, and she left unexpectedly the same day as the incident at the coffee shop. No one admitted knowing why.

Benjamin Lunce wasn't a volunteer at the ranch, but he used to come by to work on the machinery when it needed repair or service. He would also come by sometime just to hang around. None of the volunteers liked him. The Millers thought he still worked for an outfit out of San Marcos, a city about an hour away. At first, he handled warranty issues for a tractor the Millers had purchased in San Marcos. He seemed good at what he did, so the Millers continued giving him business. They were unaware of the animosity the volunteers had toward Lunce.

The only person who volunteered anything about Lunce was a guy named Donny. I didn't catch his last name. He said that Frances was frightened of Lunce, but that he had only learned of her fear of Lunce the day before she left.

During the group interview, a new deputy came in and talked to Deputy Stephens for a second.

"I need all the volunteers to go with Deputy Samson and this young deputy here. We have a van that will transport you to the sheriff's office, where we'll need to get your statements. The same van will bring you back here later today. Deputy Cooper and I will stay here to get your statements." Stephens directed his last comment toward the two owners.

He walked Lieutenant Martin and me back outside.

"What do you think?" he asked Martin.

"I think we have a lot more to run with than what we had yesterday at this time. I imagine when you have the volunteers separated and individually interviewed, you'll get additional details."

"That's the game plan. I'll keep you informed, Marty."

"Lieutenant, did the guy who broke into the Scott warehouse last night have a connection here?" I asked.

"I doubt it. He's a loser. Third time we've got him on minor theft charges in the last two years. This time he may actually serve time behind bars."

"You got his name?" Deputy Stephens asked. "I'll check him with Simon and Bell."

"I'll get it to you in a minute. It's Mike something or other, but I guess I ought to get it straight before I pass it on to you. Are you going to ask them additional questions about Wally?"

"Yeah, and, of course, considerably more on Ms. Wilikin. I'll fax you copies of all the statements late today."

"Thanks. The sheriff going to be all right with all that?" Martin asked.

"What he doesn't know won't hurt him."

The two shook hands, and in minutes we were back on the road to Fredericksburg.

"That was interesting," I said. "Why do you think Frances developed such a fear of Lunce?"

"That is the big question. She may have said something to one of the other volunteers."

"Guess she could have said something to Wally, but that won't do us any good unless he confided it to someone else."

"True again. Do you have any answers to go along with these questions?" he asked.

"This communal life, it's not like a cult or something is it? Maybe they wouldn't let her go away."

"No. Everyone is familiar with the Millers and their taking in young volunteers. Other than a couple of the volunteers getting busted for something minor over the years, I've never heard anything derogatory about the operations or life there at the place."

"I didn't get the feeling any of them were nervous about being there, either. Any of them could have overpowered the old couple," I said.

"At least we know who our victim was," he said, referring to the one person found in his jurisdiction, Benjamin Lunce.

"Our victim?" I asked.

"Ha! By the way, are you trying to get something going with Officer Morris?"

His question surprised me. "What?"

"You asked her out to dinner the first night you met her, then last night you kept her out drinking. I suggest you go carefully there."

I couldn't tell if he was pulling my leg or was serious. He kept a poker face as he took another bend in the road too fast.

"Lieutenant, I'm not trying to get something going with Officer Morris. In fact, I'm beginning to think all the women in this town are out of my league," I said.

That made him smile. "They probably are. Seriously, though, one man to another, Officer Morris has about every belt they can hand out in judo, or ju-jitsu, or whatever they call that martial arts stuff these days. So be sure you get permission before you try to touch."

I still couldn't tell if he was being serious or not. "She's safe with me," I finally said.

"I just don't need any more guys coming in complaining

about their broken fingers."

I guessed those fingers went somewhere they weren't invited. I planned to keep mine under control.

When we got back to Highway 290, I noticed a sign mentioning a wildflower farm. "What's with the flower farm?" I asked.

"We've got tons of wild flowers that grow down here in the spring. Quite nice, especially the bluebonnets. You're here at the wrong time of year."

"So the wildflower farm is a place you can go and see them year round?" I asked. I remembered the tulip fields in Holland that I had visited with my wife years back. Not one of those things that I had included on my list of things to do in Europe; however, I found myself impressed with the place.

"If you're into flowers," Martin said, raising his eyebrows.

"Maybe if I come back again sometime."

"There's actually a lot of things to do around here. There's a bat cave not far from here. People go there at sunset to watch the bats come out. Kind of neat."

"Bats?" I asked.

"Yes, you know. Those are the little bird-like creatures with fangs."

"I know."

Chapter 10

I considered driving to San Antonio. The ninety-minute drive would do me good and would get me away from Fredericksburg for a while. Despite my troubles the last time I visited San Antonio, I've always enjoyed my visits there.

Unfortunately, someone invented the cell phone, and for some reason we all think we have to have one these days. Two texts arrived on my phone within seconds of each other and messed up my escape plans. The first came from Sylvia, who said she really wanted to see me today. She gave no explanation. The second came from Tom. He said he had some information about Wally's murder and claimed he couldn't take it to the police yet. He wanted to see me today, too, and invited me to his house for a lunch at one.

I called Sylvia, and my call went immediately into voicemail. I left her a message that said I was tied up from noon to three, but then I was free. I also sent Tom a text saying I'd be there at one. While I waited for a response from Sylvia, I took advantage of the washer and dryer in the hotel. I no longer had any confidence in leaving Fredericksburg any time soon.

I received a text response from Sylvia that said after three would be fine. She would be at her office until six. I didn't receive any additional message from Tom. At twelve-thirty, I got in my car and headed to his place. While I had been happy to see Tom and Brenda on Saturday, the drama between them had gotten old.

To my surprise, a small group of people greeted me upon my arrival at the Hasben's. Although it wasn't as big a group as they had had for their grand opening, I still counted five other people there besides Tom and Brenda. Bull and Torry Durham greeted me like an old friend. Theo and Angie Dill reintroduced themselves and seemed cordial, but more aloof than the Durhams.

I remembered that Bull and Torry owned a ranch or farm next to the Hasbens. While I hadn't remembered Theo's and Angie's last name, I recalled they owned a car dealership in Fredericksburg. The fifth guy was the young man who had been there briefly for the grand opening. I hadn't been introduced at the opening, and his greeting to me consisted only of a nod.

There appeared to be a reluctance to talk about the murders. Since I didn't know if the presence of the rest of the people had anything to do with what Tom said he wanted to talk to me about, I didn't bring the topic up.

Tom and Brenda served grilled hamburgers and barbeque beans. Once again, their food was delicious. Other than Angie, everyone had seconds.

"Jim," Tom said, finally bringing the gathering to order. "The rest of us have been talking about the murders of Frances Wilikin and Wally Montrose. I asked them to share what they know with you."

I looked at the group. No one looked like they had any real interest in telling me anything.

"Why me instead of the police?"

"I don't think what I have is that significant," Bull Durham said.

"I'd like to keep my name out of the investigation. I have my business and my family to think about," Theo Dill said.

"I explained to them that you were an old hand at all this and had a lot more expertise in these matters than the local police," Tom said.

I didn't think my abilities were any better than those of the sheriff's office or the Fredericksburg PD, but I had learned long ago to let witnesses talk when they wanted to. I looked at the man whose name I still didn't know.

"I don't think I caught your name," I said.

"I'm Larry," he said and stuck out his hand.

"Jim West," I said and shook his hand.

"Sorry, Jim. We thought you were introduced at the opening," Brenda said.

"That's okay. Now what can I do for you?"

"I guess we're really just looking for advice," Tom said. "Theo, why don't you go first?"

"Ok, but I don't have much to tell," Theo said and took a deep breath. "Frances came into the dealership about a week ago and asked about a receptionist position that had come open. She seemed to be a very happy young woman. She mentioned to me, when I asked her why she wanted the job, that she would be getting married soon. She told me that she and her fiancé had decided that until they had children, they would both work and save their money."

"Makes good sense," I said.

"A couple of days later, I had my secretary send her an email telling her she could have the job and to come in to start work this past Monday. She called me personally last Friday to say that she had messed everything up and that she couldn't take the job. I thought she might be crying, so I asked her if everything was okay. She said no and claimed there was nothing anyone could do to help her. She said that she just needed to get away for a while."

"But no further explanation?" I asked.

"No, nothing at all. I thought something might have happened between her and her fiancé."

Even if I disagreed with Theo's decision not to talk to the police, I could understand why he thought what he knew wasn't significant. I looked at Bull Durham and then at Larry.

"I guess I'll go next," Bull said. "We never met that girl, but I knew Wally fairly well. I know he really flipped over her. He was on cloud nine until this past Saturday."

"The day she was kidnapped," I said.

"Yes."

"Did he know she was kidnapped that day?"

"No," Bull said. "He didn't know about it when he talked to me, and that was late in the day. Maybe around seven in the evening, he stopped by to talk to me about a small project I needed him to do. I could tell right away something wasn't right and asked him what was going on. He didn't hesitate to tell me. He said Frances, who I assumed was his fiancée, was fleeing town."

"Those were his words?" I asked.

"Yes, fleeing town. She told him she had really screwed everything up. She didn't tell him specifically what she had done, but that she had trusted someone who had betrayed her. Wally told me that she claimed she had to leave for her own safety and for his. She sincerely believed they were both in danger. She said once she found some place safe, she would get in touch with him. He could join her, if he still wanted to be with her."

"Did Wally understand what she meant by that?"

"No. He was one confused young man. He pleaded with her to stay. He said he told her that he would protect her. She said she couldn't put him in that much danger, especially now that she didn't even deserve him anymore. He had no idea what she was talking about. After crying for a while, she fell asleep on his bed. She stayed the night with him. He fell asleep next to her, and when he awoke Saturday morning, she was gone."

"I thought she stayed out at the ranch."

"Wally claimed it was very rare for her not to go back to the ranch each night, but that night she claimed she was afraid to. In the morning, Wally tried to call her, but she never answered her phone. He finally called the Millers and was told that Frances had just left. They thought she had gone for good."

"Anything else?" I asked.

"Yes, and I feel bad about not telling this to the police earlier. She warned Wally that if he was ever approached by Ben Lunce, that he needed to be careful. She instructed him to tell Lunce that he had no idea where she had gone."

"It turned out she was right to be afraid of Lunce. Was there anyone else?"

"Wally said that she was evasive on that question, but that she appeared to only be afraid of Lunce. I had the feeling that Wally believed there had to be another person besides Lunce."

"Did Wally say anything about going to see Lunce to find out what this was all about?"

"Yeah, yeah, he did. Do you think it was Wally who killed Lunce?" Bull asked me.

"Very likely."

"Jim, that's all I know about any of this. Torry and I have prayed over all this. I hope I haven't caused anyone's death by remaining silent."

I guessed his guilt was only over Wally's death. He couldn't have foreseen the first incident, and like the rest of us, didn't have much sympathy for the second victim.

"Anything more?" I asked Tom.

"Larry has something to add."

I looked at Larry. He didn't seem to like eye contact. "I don't really know anything," he said. "I didn't know you wanted me to tell anyone about what I said yesterday evening when you invited me to lunch, Mr. Hasben."

"I'm sorry if we put you on the spot, Larry. It was more my idea than Tom's," Brenda said. "I think it could be important."

"It's just that everyone will think I'm prejudiced," Larry said.

"About what?" I asked.

"It's just that the only guy I've ever seen Ben hang around with was a black guy from San Antonio. They used to go over there now and then. I thought for sure I saw that girl, Frances, that's her name, right, Mr. Hasben?"

Tom nodded.

"Well, I thought I saw her in Lunce's old truck heading toward Austin in the middle of last week. That black guy was in the truck with them."

"Did she look afraid?"

"Not that I noticed. They looked normal. I just wondered why she was hanging around Lunce. I didn't really know the guy, but I had heard he had a bad reputation with the ladies."

"Why do you think they were going to Austin and not some

city in between?" I asked.

"Guess I don't really know. They were just heading in that direction."

I asked one more time for anything else, but they all claimed that they knew nothing else.

"This is information that really needs to go to the police," I said.

"Come on, I was afraid of this," Theo whined to Tom.

"Does it have to come from us?" Torry asked me.

"What I can do is talk to the authorities and try to keep your names out of it. I can't promise anything. Bottom line, you may, at some point, have to talk to them yourselves. They can protect your identity better than I can."

"Will you do your best?" Tom asked.

"Yes."

"Can't you look into this by yourself?" We'd be happy to hire you," Brenda said.

Bull nodded in support of the idea.

"No. I'm not licensed, I don't have the knowledge base for the area, and I've retired from all that." The last bit was a stretch. In the handful of years since I retired, I'd been sucked into more murder investigations than I'd seen in my twenty years in the Air Force. I didn't like the idea of being sucked any further into these three.

"Okay," Bull said. "Do what you can for us. We're in your debt for just doing that. This killing has to come to a stop."

"I will," I said.

The gathering broke up after that. Larry left while the ladies were clearing the table. I sensed Bull and Torry wanted to stay and visit for a while. I didn't want to stay, so I said my farewells and left. I also got Larry's last name, Poole, from Tom. It was a loose end that I didn't like hanging out there.

I never had much sympathy for people who "don't want to get involved." Problems don't get fixed, and people often get hurt, because someone didn't want to get involved. There's a mile-wide gap between being a busybody and just getting involved. It's too bad people don't get it. I'd be a rich man if I got a dollar for every time someone, after we had solved a case, told me that they knew something wasn't quite right. It was bad enough after a suicide when some witness would inevitably step forward crying about how he or she knew that the person was going to kill themselves one day. The worst, though, came after a child's death from abuse.

On the drive back to town, I tried to digest the information and mesh it with what I already knew. I didn't come up with any answers, but I believed the information could help fill in some of the gaps in the investigation. By now, the deputies could've finished interviewing the six volunteers, so I decided to go see Lieutenant Martin before calling Sylvia. I arrived at the Law Enforcement Center at two-thirty. A uniformed desk officer told me the Lieutenant could be found at the substation by the court house.

I drove to the middle of town. I'd been to the substation once before. An officer loitering by the front desk got the task of walking me to the Lieutenant's office. I found myself looking around for Cat, but she didn't appear to be in.

"What's up, West?" Martin asked.

"First, I want to make it clear I haven't been out trying to dig anything up on the shootings. I had lunch a little while ago with a few of your local citizens. They got to talking about the murders. They shared a couple of tidbits of information. I thought you should know what they said."

"Why don't they come and talk to us?" the Lieutenant asked.

"I told them they should. They'd rather not, but they said it was okay for me to bring you the information. My guess is that the lunch was set up so they could tell me what they knew, and I could share it with you."

"With the few people you know in this town, it wouldn't be much of a challenge to find out who these people are."

"I know," I said. "None of this is my idea, but I figured at this point getting the information to you was the important thing."

"What do you have? No, wait a second." He picked up his phone, punched a few buttons, and told someone to send Officer Morris in.

In the four minutes it took Cat to reach his office from wherever she was, Martin complained about how this investigation was going to make him miss the weeklong hunting trip he had planned with a cousin.

She greeted me with a warm smile and shook my hand when she came into his office.

"Are we finally going to be able to arrest this guy, Lieutenant?" she asked.

"Sit down, Cat. West has something to tell us, and your being here will prevent him or me from repeating his story."

For the next twenty minutes, I briefed the two of them on what I had learned at lunch. They had the usual comments and questions, but I couldn't tell them anymore than what I knew.

"You know, Jim, if the jerk who knew Wally was out looking

for Lunce had told us that at the time, we might have been able to at least prevent him from being killed."

"I know, Lieutenant." I also knew he was referring to Wally's death as the one they might have been able to prevent. I had the idea that no one in the room cared much about Lunce's death, other than they now had an additional investigation that needed to be resolved.

"Cat, we need to find out who this black guy is. He may or may not have anything to do with the killings, but right now he may be the only person who can fill in the rest of the gaps."

"I'll get on it right away, sir," she said.

"You'll need to brief Stephens on this info, too."

"Have you learned anything from the interviews of the volunteers?" I asked.

Rather than answer me, Martin turned to Cat. "Take West with you and call Stephens. You can use the office upstairs."

We left together. I was a little irritated that Martin chose to ignore my question. Cat must have sensed my irritation.

"Don't get grumpy on me. He doesn't want to be the one to share the info with you. He doesn't want to have to look the Chief or the Sheriff in the eye and lie to him if all this hits the fan some day."

That made sense. I knew the two didn't get along.

"I'm surprised your chief isn't a little more involved in this matter," I said.

"Don't be. He's in Oregon burying his mother."

"Oh, sorry." I felt awkward. "My curiosity prompted my comment, not a desire to be critical of the Chief."

"Don't worry about it."

"I understand you know a thing or two about judo," I said to change the topic.

"It's a hobby. Who told you?"

"Just someone who wanted me to behave around you."

She gave me a look that implied she had no idea what I was talking about. I wondered why I even brought the topic up. I didn't feel right telling her that her boss had a conversation about her with me.

"Don't worry. I'm not going to challenge you to a match. I don't know why I even brought that up, either."

She let the conversation pass. We entered a small office that looked like it was rarely used. Cat set the small briefcase she had been carrying on a desk and opened it. She removed a stack of paper and handed it to me.

"Copies of the statements they took from the group that works the Millers' place. There are also copies of the two statements provided by the Millers. You can't keep them, but you can read them. Other than providing some interesting info on Lunce, they really don't say much."

I read through the statements while Cat fiddled with her smart phone. It didn't take long. They all acknowledged that something happened in the past week that had frightened Frances into believing she had to leave. She had not confided to any of them the basis for her sudden fear. Both young women volunteers claimed that Benjamin Lunce was a lecher. He gave them the creeps, but other than his overall behavior around them when he happened to get one of them alone, they could offer no specifics.

"What do you think?" I asked Cat when I finished reading.

"How about you tell me what you think," she responded.

Fair enough, I thought. They had shared the statements

with me. "I think something happened to Frances last week. Lunce likely was behind whatever happened, if he didn't do whatever it was himself. I think she was fleeing Lunce and his associates when I saw her Saturday morning. She was too embarrassed or ashamed to tell Wally what exactly happened, but she said enough to convince Wally that Lunce was involved. I'm not sure if Lunce killed Frances, but if he didn't, he took her to the person who did. My guess is that Wally killed Lunce in an act of revenge."

"That leaves the question who killed Wally and why?" Cat said.

"Exactly. If you can identify Lunce's associate or associates, I think you'll have a chance at identifying the last shooter. Did they find any evidence out at the scene where we think the person fired at Wally?"

"No. No shell casings, cigarette butts, footprints, etc. The ground is hard out there and there's a hard dirt road near the site. They didn't develop anything."

"Too bad. Were my guesses anywhere close to yours?"

"Pretty much on. Both the county and we have sent leads to Austin PD to try to track down Lunce's activities and connections there. The same leads have been sent to every other town within a hundred-mile radius. Even though the kidnapping case turned into a murder investigation, the FBI is still monitoring our efforts and providing us access to anything we need."

"Sounds like it's just good old investigative work from here on out. You shouldn't need me here anymore."

"I think I would've enjoyed working on a ranch when I was younger," she said.

The comment came out of the blue. I couldn't tell if she was ignoring my statement, or if this was a topic she really wanted to get into. There might have been a time when working at a communal ranch might have appealed to me, but looking back I couldn't remember when that would have been.

"I don't know if it's as romantic as you might think."

"Had to be as romantic as my own life was when I was the same age of most of those kids. It would have been an adventure."

"Like the hippies of old?" I said.

"Some people still want to live that lifestyle," she said.

I remembered a trip I took to Whidbey Island in Washington not too long ago. It appeared to me that many of the hippies of northern California had migrated up there and were still trying to hang onto their culture.

"Do you know the Millers?" I asked, not sure why the thought of the old timer hippies in Washington brought my focus back to the Millers.

"Not really. I think I've met them once or twice, but I'm not even sure of that. Why do you ask, Jim?"

"Everyone is convinced they're super clean. When so many people think like that about anyone, it always bothers me. Over the years, I've discovered that most people have at least a few demons in their past."

"I'm sure the sheriff is looking at them," she said. "I know they're also trying to track down some of the past volunteers. They might have something in their past, but like I said, I haven't heard anything negative about them."

"Good. Any suspicions that any of them held back something significant?" I pointed at the copies of the statements.

"The volunteers?"

"Uh huh," I mumbled in the affirmative.

"That's always a possibility, but I don't have anything specific to corroborate any doubts. You know something we don't?"

"No. Wish I did. Nothing would make me happier than to have this whole mess over."

"I'll talk to the Lieutenant about letting you go home. There are a few more restaurants in town I'd like to show you, Jim, but I know we have no right to keep you here much longer."

"Thanks," I said.

"By the way, do these people who confided in you today at lunch expect you to get back to them?"

"They might, but I'm not going to. If they contact me, I'll let them know I passed on what they told me to you all and tell them again they should deal directly with you. Can I give them your name?"

"Of course," she said.

She walked me out to the front sidewalk.

"Say, Jim, what are the demons in your past?"

"What?" I asked.

"You said inside that very few people haven't any demons in their past. You said it like you were no exception."

"That's right. I try to keep mine buried deep and under control. I learned long ago it doesn't do you any good to bring them out into the light of day. And you?"

"Mine still scare me," she said without elaborating.

"You take care of yourself, Cat," I said. We shook hands, and I left.

I had only taken a dozen or so steps toward my car when the

hair on the back of my neck started twitching. I had the sudden sense that someone was watching me. My peripheral vision had caught it, but it took a couple seconds for the rest of me to confirm it. A hooded figure stood across the street partially concealed by the corner of a building. I looked at the figure, and it stared back at me.

Chapter 11

I stopped walking and looked over at the person. With the hood of the sweatshirt pulled up over his head, I couldn't tell who it was. Paranoia, I thought, and started to turn away when the person signaled to me with a hand. The signal definitely indicated that the person wanted me to come across the street to him. He repeated the signal before ducking further behind the edge of the building.

Cat had disappeared back into the building. I debated whether to cross the street or not. Curiosity, rather than logic, won out. I crossed over and rounded the corner of the building. An alley stretched between buildings to the next street. Halfway down the alley, the figure in the hoodie leaned against the wall of one of the buildings.

As I approached the person, I realized the he was a she, and she looked familiar.

"You're not actually a cop, are you?" she asked. She was one of the two young women volunteers I had seen that morning.

"No, I'm not. What can I do for you?"

"Can we go somewhere to talk?" she asked.

"Yes, but what do you want from me? Weren't you just interviewed at the Sheriff's office?"

"Please."

"Okay, are you hungry? There's a hamburger place down the block," I said.

She stuck close to my side with her head down looking at the ground while we walked the short distance to the fast food restaurant.

"Are you afraid of something?" I asked.

"No, but I don't want to be seen talking to you."

"Well, this place isn't going to be that private."

"It'll have to do."

Once inside, she led me to a far corner table and sat facing away from the front entrance. Before I sat down, I noticed we would have to order our food at the counter.

"What can I get you?"

"A Coke and an order of fries, if you don't mind," she said. She didn't look around.

I ordered fries for both of us and returned to the table with her Coke and a sweet tea for myself. "They'll bring us the fries in about four minutes they said. Now, please, tell me again your name and what's going on."

"I'm Glo, just G-L-O, no W." I remembered that her name was Gloria Banks. "There was no way I was going to tell them this morning what I know. I thought I would tell someone at the Fredericksburg police station, since they're also investigating the murders. If I said anything this morning, everyone would know it was me. I don't need any trouble."

"Then why talk to me instead of the police?"

"That was my good luck. You can pass on what I tell you. That way I can look everyone in the eye and truthfully deny that I told the cops anything more than Lunce was a jerk."

What was going on? I felt like someone had painted a big sign that floated around with me that said "Forget the police, talk to me!"

"Anything you tell me I would have to pass on to the police," I said.

"That's okay. I want you to. You can even give them my

name, but I won't talk to them, at least not right now."

A short, heavy teenager with a bad case of acne on his face and a Texas Rangers baseball cap on his head arrived with our fries. I took the brief break in our conversation to decide how I should handle the situation. Although I didn't like the position I found myself in for the second time today, I didn't think I had much of a choice if I wanted to hear what she had to say.

"Before we get started, Glo, I need to send someone a short text. It won't mention you."

"Sure."

I sent Sylvia a note saying that I was running late.

"All right, Glo, tell me what you want me to know, and I'll share it with Officer Morris. She works in the building I just came out of and is involved with the investigation. I'll try to make her understand your predicament, but first I need you to help me understand your situation along with whatever information you provide. Does that sound fair?"

"Yes. I know that Ben Lunce worked with a pimp in Austin. I don't think he was a pimp, but he was connected to one. He procured women for the pimp. He was trying to provide Frances to his pimp buddy."

"Okay, hold on a second. How do you know all this?"

"I haven't exactly had the perfect life. What's your name?"

"West, Jim West. Call me Jim, please."

"Not to bore you with all the details, but I spent a lot of time in foster homes. After that, I spent a couple of years on the streets before a man helped me get straight. I'm trying to get a handle on my life right now. The Millers and their ranch are the best things that ever happened to me, other than Allister. I warned Frances, but she was too innocent to understand that there really is a Satan, and he's always out there."

"How did you learn about Lunce and the pimp?" I asked, trying to keep pace with her rapid remarks. I also didn't want to get unto a discussion about Satan.

"I didn't know for sure until the morning Frances left. I suspected it ever since Loretta disappeared shortly after I arrived at the ranch in February."

"Loretta was a volunteer there?"

"Yes."

"And she disappeared?"

"One day she didn't come home from a shopping trip in Austin. She caught the morning bus on her day off. She didn't return. The next day a guy shows up saying he's a cousin. He claims he's looking for her because another relative had passed away, and he thought she might want to attend the funeral. That night Bell, Mrs. Miller, gets an email allegedly from Loretta saying that she has to go home to a funeral and may not be back. She said that her possessions could be given to charity or to us. She no longer wanted them."

"Why do you say allegedly?"

"Two reasons," Glo said. "First, one thing Loretta left behind was a small unicorn statue that meant a lot to her. That didn't make sense to me. I also knew that Lunce had been hitting on her, and for some stupid reason, she didn't seem to mind. When this guy who claimed to be her cousin dropped by, Lunce happened to be working on the old truck that we use on the ranch. I saw the two make eye contact. They knew each other."

"Did you tell anyone about your concerns?"

"No. I had no proof, and I was new there."

"Did he hit on you?"

"Yes, but I told him to stay the hell away from me," she said.

"Did he?"

"Yeah, I think he sensed that I knew what he was doing. You live on the streets and hang out with the walking dead long enough, you can tell."

"Walking dead?" All I could think of was the television show and zombies.

"Could as well have been. That's what you are out there."

I fought the urge to ask her about her past. "How does all this fit in with Frances?"

"Shortly after she arrived Lunce focused his attention on her. He was only around once or twice a week, and Frances thought he was harmless. She never was attracted to the guy, but she thought he was funny and never saw the danger. I warned her more than once, but she didn't take me seriously. When she got engaged, I stopped worrying about her. I didn't even know she went to Austin until I heard she came back. She was scared to death and ready to run."

"How do you know Lunce was involved?"

"She didn't want to talk about it. Something bad happened to her, but she didn't say, and I didn't ask. Somehow she had gotten away. She wouldn't tell me where she was going."

"But you think Lunce was involved?" I asked again.

"That was all she said. She told me I was right. She said over and over that she should have listened to me. She didn't want to talk about what happened, and I didn't want to press it. I did tell her to at least tell Wally or her parents where she was going. She said she would, but at the time she didn't know herself."

"Did she mention Lunce's name or anyone else's?"

"No. I didn't want to know who they were. Can't you figure out why I didn't want to talk to the deputies? Why I decided to talk to you rather than the police?"

She was scared. I could tell. Despite her street knowledge, or perhaps because of it, she was very frightened.

"Why do you think they killed her?"

"She must have seen something or someone. I don't know. They usually just beat you, threaten your family, and put you back out on the street. You're a commodity to them," she said.

"But they didn't own her yet," I said.

"I know. That's why she must have seen something or someone."

"Did Lunce know Wally Montrose?"

"I imagine they may have met at some time, but I don't think they really knew each other. I'm glad he's dead. Lunce, I mean."

"Did you and Frances share a room at the Miller place?" I asked.

"No. I lucked into a small private room. Not much more than a small storage room, but it's just mine."

I could see something flicker in Glo's eyes when she spoke about her room.

"Did Frances have a room of her own?"

"Not really. She hadn't been here that long. At first, Wendy roomed with her."

"Wendy?"

"She's the other girl. Well, Frances hadn't been here a month, and Wendy moved in with Toby out in the barn. Sean moved in with Steve to make room for Wendy."

"So Frances shared a room with an absent roommate," I said.

"For the most part. Every now and then Wendy and Toby would have an argument, but those two never stayed apart more than a day or two," Glo said.

"Would Wendy know anything about this?"

"I don't think so. She's kind of focused on herself."

That brought a grin to my face. "How about you, Glo? Are you really all right?"

"A little frightened, but I'm okay."

"How'd you get your life turned around?"

"I had help. I don't think I could've done it on my own. I don't like to think about those days." She ate the last of her French fries and took a sip of her Coke.

"Want a refill?" I asked.

She shook her head. "Allister saved me. He just came along one night and saved me." I thought I could see the same flicker of light in her eyes that I had when she mentioned her own room. "He said he had seen me a few times before. I hadn't noticed him. When he saw me that night, he said his heart broke, and he just had to take me home."

"Were you homeless?"

"And worse. A lot worse. Allister took me to his downtown condo. I lived, if that's what you can call it, in Dallas at the time. He had a house in Grapevine, but he also had a condo in the city. He told me that it was time for me to start my life over. He told me that I now had the job as his condo's live-in caretaker. I remember thinking that this was just another person who was going to use me, hurt me, maybe even kill me, but I didn't care. At the time, I think I truly wanted to die."

"But it wasn't like that?"

She shook her head again. "The first night has always been a bit vague in my mind. When he picked me up, I might have been high, drunk, or both. I think I had already started to go insane. He told me to take a shower and put me to bed. I know he didn't do anything to me. I slept forever. I think it was only sixteen hours, but he always teased me about sleeping a day and a half."

"What was he doing with you?" I still had my doubts. He wouldn't have been the first man who wanted his own possession.

"I didn't care, and it confused me at first. He didn't behave like anyone else I ever knew."

"No sex?" I asked.

"Sex?" Now I made her laugh. "Of course we had sex, but not then, not at first. Not for a couple of days. That's what I didn't understand. He didn't push me for anything at first. For a couple of days, he would not leave to go to work until I was awake, and he felt it was safe to leave me. I don't know what he thought I might do. I was always free to leave. He returned at night each day after his work. Maybe the third or fourth day I was there, after he came home from work, we went out for a pizza. That's the first time I think my head was really clear. We talked, and he told me he was serious about having me take care of the condo. He would be spending most of his time at his house. He claimed he would feel better if someone would look after his condo when he wasn't there."

"Was he married?"

"Separated. When we got home from the pizza, I still assumed I had to pay him with my body. He pushed me away and made it very clear again that I didn't owe him sex for anything he had done. That if we evolved into a sexual relationship, it would be because we both wanted it to, not because I owed him a thing."

"Was he serious?" I asked.

"Yes. I kept looking for the trap. There wasn't one."

"Sounds too good to be true."

"I know. I didn't really care at the time. I mostly slept. After I'd been there five or six days, I thought I should make a run for it. He had actually bought me some clothes, so I could have something to new to wear. I put them in a trash bag and had my hand on the door knob to leave when I realized how absurd it would be to leave. If I was going to run off and escape, where could I go that was any safer or better than where I was?"

"What did you do?"

"I took a hot bath. When Allister came home that night, I asked him what he really wanted."

"Did he tell you?"

"In his way, he did. His main motivation for taking me out of the cesspool I lived in had been a noble one. He wanted to save me. Looking back, I have no doubt about that. It's really no different than the person who finds a wet puppy on the side of the road. They pick it up and take it home. They rescue it. My taking care of his condo was only the scenario he had in his mind to give me something to do and to keep me off the streets."

"You were his puppy?" I asked.

"Yes. That I was." She smiled. "I made him sleep with me that night. He kept saying 'Only if you want to.' Days later, I finally got him to admit that he had wanted to sleep with me from the moment he first got me into his car. He was so embarrassed after he admitted it. For days afterwards, he kept telling me his primary motivation was to help me."

"Think it was?"

"You know, I don't care if it was or if it wasn't. He treated me with kindness, and it's what he wanted to believe. We had what I think was a fairly normal relationship, other than how it got started. I doubt if most relationships start with one person finding their future partner homeless, smelly, dirty, and overall disgusting."

"What happened?"

"His wife came back. They had been separated, not divorced. She had moved out to Phoenix with a job a couple of years earlier. They had a big falling out over careers and marriage. The separation was serious, not just one caused by geography. They didn't visit each other. He never talked about it much. I didn't care to know the details, although she made them clear to me when she returned."

"I'm sorry."

"Don't be. The doorbell rang one morning a few minutes after Allister went to work. She had returned. I recognized her from a photo I had found in a drawer. She told me to pack up and get out of her condo. At first I got angry, but mostly I was confused. She didn't get nasty with me. She approached the whole thing rather businesslike. She assumed I was an employee at the advertising company where Allister worked who had made the move on her husband once she was gone."

"So she didn't know anything about your background?"

"No. She had been in Dallas long enough to see me hanging

around the condo, but she hadn't talked to Allister. She didn't seem to be mad at Allister for our relationship. The separation was on its third year. I imagine she had an affair or two in Phoenix. She had come to the condo to get me out. That was her first goal. Get rid of me, and then try to get Allister back for herself."

"So what did you do?"

"I left. She made it an easy decision. The condo security people were on the way up to throw me out. The condo was still in both their names. In an effort to show me she wasn't totally heartless, she said I could stay in her hotel room. She planned to move into the condo that day, and she had already paid for two more nights at the hotel."

"And Allister welcomed her back?"

"Yes. I don't know how quickly, but he did. Allister came to the hotel to see me. He was almost in tears, terrified that I would return to the streets. He kept saying he loved me, but he loved his wife, too."

"Did he?" I asked before I could check myself.

"Love me? I'm sure he did. After all, I was his puppy that he found on the side of a road. More importantly, he told me about this place, the Millers' ranch. I came here on a bus ticket he paid for, not knowing if I'd stay or not, but I needed to get out of Dallas."

"It's worked out okay here for you, right?" I asked.

"Yes, very much so. I'm sorry I talked so much. Other than Bell, I haven't told anyone my story since Allister. I guess it's just that I had to tell someone about Lunce. Maybe I felt you wouldn't believe me if I didn't tell you why I was so sure. Like I said, I can smell his type from a mile away."

"I believe you, Glo. I'll pass along the information to Officer Morris. I heard that Lunce had a black friend who might have driven with Lunce and Frances to Austin the day or two before she tried to make her run. Can you remember any black male acquaintance that Benjamin Lunce might have had?"

"No. I don't know any acquaintance he had. I never saw him with a black man. I also thought Frances drove herself to Austin."

That was news to me. However, it fit a piece of the puzzle that was trying to form in my mind.

"Do you know a guy named Cappy or Hank Stewart?" I asked.

"No. I don't think I've ever even heard of either name before."

She didn't have more to add about the investigation, and I couldn't think of any more questions. We sat and talked for a while about life on the Millers' ranch. She truly seemed to be very happy there. I offered her a ride back if she needed one, but she said she had a ride with one of the guys who had a few errands to run. They had agreed to meet at six to head back. That gave her twenty minutes to do some window-shopping. She didn't want to be seen leaving with me, so we said our goodbyes inside, and she left first. When I walked outside a minute or two later, she had already disappeared.

I dialed Sylvia, but my call went directly into voice mail. I left her a message saying that it had been a crazy day, that I was now available, and for her to call me back. I stared across the street. For the umpteenth time in the past few days, I walked into the police station. The desk sergeant gave me a strange look and said that Officer Morris had left for the day. He added that she was on call, and he could reach her if necessary. I told him it could wait until tomorrow. I knew the information would be helpful, but I also felt reluctant to drag her back into work.

Chapter 12

"What have you been doing with yourself all day?" Sylvia asked after my arrival at her office.

"It's been a crazy day. Are you familiar with the Millers' ranch south of here?" I asked.

"Sure. Everyone knows about the ranch. How come?" she asked.

"The first victim, Frances Wilikin, lived there. Her attacker, Benjamin Lunce, worked on the machinery there now and then."

"Really? I don't think I've ever heard anything bad about the place," she said.

"I don't think any of this has anything to do with the ranch, other than that's where she worked and that's where the two met."

"That's good. I've suggested to a few friends who have had nieces, nephews or cousins that seemed to be messed up, that the Millers' ranch might be a good place for them."

"Do they cater to those with issues?" I asked.

"Not that I know of, but I've always thought of it as a place where a person could get away from their problems. Several years ago, I met a guy who worked there. He had taken a year off after getting out of the military before going back to college. A real nice guy, he said he needed a year of working in the sun to get rid of the little gremlins that had tried to set up residence in his mind."

"I hope he succeeded," I said.

"I like to think that he did. He left to attend some school back East."

I told Sylvia what I had learned during the day without telling her who had talked to me. She didn't seem to have any curiosity in knowing my sources, but the information had her tantalized.

"What do you think happened to poor Frances?" she asked when I finished.

"I could only speculate."

"I don't want to," she said, but I could tell that's exactly what Sylvia was churning around in her brain. "Poor girl. Think she saw something that got her killed?"

"I guess it's possible. I mean, unless we can come up with a better explanation it may be the best guess we have. There are a few gaps and a few discrepancies that need to be resolved. However, that's normal. The police must feel that they're chipping away at the final solution." I said.

"When they hear the latest you've learned, I think they'll solve this whole thing in a few days. Don't you think?" she asked.

"I hope so."

She gave me a hug and a short kiss on the lips. "I wanted to talk to you because I've really enjoyed being with you. I know you need to go home. I'll miss you. I really will. I asked you to come here because I needed to get this inventory done, and tonight looked like the best time to do it." She paused for a few seconds, and I could tell she was trying to decide how to tell me something. "Jerry Stephens called me today. He wants to take me out to dinner tomorrow."

"That's great," I said, and I meant it. "I've already stayed longer than I meant to. I even had to wash my clothes today." I paused for a second and looked at Sylvia. "I'm serious when I say that it's great that Stephens wants to take you out."

"I think so, too, but I don't want you to have the wrong impression of me."

"I don't. I don't even understand why I should have a wrong impression."

"You won't mind, if you're still here, that I would go out with him?"

"Of course not," I said. "But I will mind still being here."

"Jim, I want you to understand that I really like you. If I thought you were going to stay here, like forever, I wouldn't go out with him."

"Sylvia, go out with him. I understand the situation." Of course, I've never really understood any situation I've gotten myself into with a woman. I thought I had my marriage figured out, until I came home one day, and she was gone. I'd only known Sylvia for a few days and certainly didn't feel like she owed me anything.

I stayed for an hour helping her with her inventory. We talked a little more about the investigation, but not about us. When I left, she gave me another hug and a kiss. I had the odd feeling that I had just been dumped. I also started wondering if she might have wanted me to say I didn't want her to go out with Jerry or any other man. Did she want me to get emotional and even possessive?

I stopped at a convenience store and bought one of those big cans of beer. A night in bed watching television might get my mind off what I should have said to or done with Sylvia tonight.

My car, however, decided I needed dinner and drove me

back to the Mexican restaurant I had almost eaten at the night before. Once again, I couldn't find a close in parking spot. Cars filled the restaurant's small lot, and all the spaces in front of the restaurant had been taken. I found a spot around the corner on the next cross street. Approaching the restaurant on the sidewalk, I noticed an older gentleman coming toward me.

"Doc, is that you?" I asked when we met in front of the restaurant.

He stared at me a second. He probably didn't remember me or my name. His dark suit looked as old as he was.

"I'm Jim West. I think we met on Saturday at the Hasbens' grand opening."

"Oh yes. I'm sorry. At my age, I get faces all mixed up. I do remember you though. From New Mexico, right?"

"Yes, are you heading inside?" I asked.

"Yes. On Mondays, I visit a former patient of mine who now lives in an assisted living facility on the edge of town. I guess she's not a former patient, just not a current patient. She's doing quite well these days."

"Good for her. I'm going inside, too. If you're alone, you're welcome to join me."

"I guess I could do that. Might not be the best of company for you."

"We'll be a good match then," I said. "I'm not much of a conversationalist myself."

"Ha! I guess we both need the practice. Have you eaten here before?"

"Never."

"It's a run-of-the-mill Mexican restaurant for these parts. That means the food is good and the price is cheap," he said with a grin.

"Sounds good enough by me."

A cute teenager with very dark hair, wearing glasses and a short skirt guided us to a table in the back.

"Looks like our sitting together was meant to be," he said. "Despite the late hour, I don't believe there's another empty table in the place."

"Obviously a popular place. Do you have any recommendations?"

"Hell, you only have a few choices. Any of them are fine."

I looked at the menu and saw what he meant. My choices included tacos, enchiladas, or fajitas. Of course they had to make it complicated by offering each in chicken or beef. One could even get enchiladas with just cheese. Each meal came with beans and rice. Nothing on the menu cost more than ten dollars.

"You were smart to come here," Doc said. "Not many tourists know about this place."

"Wish I felt more like a tourist," I said.

He looked at me for a second. I could see the doctor in his eyes trying to diagnose what might have made me say that.

"Feel bad about the young girl's death and its impact on the Hasbens' open house?"

"A little about the open house. Do you think the Hasbens' will succeed in their wine operation?" I asked.

He didn't answer right away. I figured he was wondering why I didn't say anything about the dead girl.

"They have a chance. Some of their wine needs to get better, but they have two good ones. That may carry them long enough to perfect the rest."

"I'm no expert on wine, but I liked them all."

"They've started off smart with six or seven standards and one special reserve wine. Down the road they'll add more wines to their inventory," he said.

"I imagine you can't produce a new wine overnight," I said.

He looked at me like he finally realized that I really didn't know much about the business of making wine. I had as much as said so to everyone since I arrived, but I guessed everyone around here had a working knowledge on the subject, so meeting a real neophyte was rare.

"They're using oak barrels, which is good, but that can make it tricky, too."

I remembered Tom showing me the barrels while I was there. I didn't know why using them could make producing wine tricky.

"Timing isn't that much of an issue as long as they stay patient. Some wines, like ports, can take two to three years to make."

"Are they making a port?" I asked.

"No, not yet. Oh, here comes help."

A waiter showed up and took our order. We both ordered the combination plate of tacos and enchiladas.

"For eight bucks, how can we go wrong?" I asked.

"That's true," he paused a second and took a sip of water. "Does that girl's death bother you?"

"Of course."

"I don't mean it the way it sounded. It's just that you ignored my question about the young woman. I didn't think you knew her."

"I didn't."

"I heard they found a dead young man the next day, too," he said.

"Yes. I think the police believe that he may have been the guy who murdered the girl."

"That's what I heard. One murder is very rare for these parts. Two in a row is unheard of," he said, shaking his head.

I wondered if I should inform him of the third. I didn't want to, but I knew he would hear about it soon. When he did, he would likely learn that I already knew about it. While it shouldn't have bothered me if he thought I held out on him, it did. "You know there was a third."

"What? A third?"

"Yes. A young man named Wally Montrose."

"What is going on? I don't think we've had but two murders in Fredericksburg in the last decade. Now we have three in as many days. Must be an outside group fighting something out on our turf."

"Could be, Doc. Right now, your guess is as good as anyone else's."

"I don't mean to imply Texas doesn't have a history of violence," he said. "We've had our Bonnie and Clydes, but it's not like your big cities down here. These small towns are relatively peaceful. I'm serious about there were only a couple murders here over the past decade."

"I believe you," I said.

"Bring in the Texas Rangers, that's what I'd do, and I don't mean the baseball team. Nowadays, everyone thinks you can solve everything by getting on the computer. You watch those TV shows?" he asked.

"Some," I didn't know exactly what shows he meant. It

could have been any of them, I thought.

"I bet you most crooks only access the computer to watch porn. Of course, you have a few intelligent criminals, but most of the crooks I've run across don't have enough brains to pull up their pants."

That made me smile. "I know what you mean."

"The Texas Rangers, they rely on good old footwork and hands-on investigating. Put them on this case, and they'll have it solved in no time," he said.

"I don't know how that works, but I imagine if the locals don't solve it soon, the Rangers will be brought in. I think the FBI is monitoring the case, too. They should be able to help out."

"The FBI has gone downhill since Hoover retired."

Doc certainly didn't need to be encouraged to voice his opinion. I didn't press the point. Hoover died long ago, and I thought the FBI still did a good job.

"Just like those young doctors out there," he continued. "They want to run everything through the computer to find an answer. Patients are becoming just another number and a paycheck, of course. The young doctors today need those computers. They dedicate half of their computer to tell them what's wrong with their patient, correct or not, and the other half to balance their stock portfolio."

The transition from old school cops to old school doctors didn't surprise me. A lot of older professionals feel like the younger ones in their profession have it a little easier or that they take too many short cuts. I know several pilots who claim flying today is nothing like flying in the "old" days. Today's planes fly themselves, they say. I also had little doubt that a lot of what the old-timers said was valid. Doc didn't have the advantage of all the resources available to a young doctor starting out in medicine today. He had to hone his skills by studying his patient. He had to do it without a computer providing him the answers.

While I could sympathize with his comments, I also knew that if a young doctor failed to use the most current resources available and misdiagnosed someone, it could cost both doctor and patient dearly. The world changes, and we adapt. Often it's for the better. We gain new knowledge and skills, but in doing so, we forget some of the old. In the world of forensic science, the investigator's ability to find blood and other bodily fluids had skyrocketed in the last thirty years. For the investigator, DNA matching, something that had only come on the scene in the past thirty years, equaled the breakthrough of penicillin in the world of medicine.

Relying solely on the evidence produced by new technologies, and ignoring the evidence developed the old-fashioned way can be a fatal mistake, too. I had no doubt the same mistakes affected the medical field as they did the investigative. I remembered too well a case where DNA supposedly exonerated a prisoner sentenced to a lengthy prison term for rape and murder years after his conviction. After his release, he killed two more young women before the authorities picked him up for the new crimes. Only then did they learn that while he had not raped the original victim, his partner had, he had been the individual who stabbed the poor woman to death.

"Have you been to any of the other wineries in the area?" Doc asked after we had about finished our dinners.

"No. Maybe on some future trip I'll check out a few."

"We've got a lot of good ones between here and Austin and a few south of that line. Becker Vineyards in Stonewall is a big one. It's well worth a visit. There are others along the highway worth checking out. If you go south a little, I'd suggest a couple around Driftwood, and then, of course, there's Dry Comal Creek in New Braunfels. It's relatively new and has some very, very good wines."

"Have to admit, you all have great names for cities down here. How can you go wrong with a name like Driftwood?" I said.

He talked for a while about specific wines he liked from the area before we finally parted company, and I headed back to the hotel.

The next morning found me once again visiting the Fredericksburg police station. Lieutenant Martin didn't want to see me until Officer Morris could join us. She had already responded to some incident that had to do with property damage and vandalism. He didn't think she would be too long. I started to wait at the station, but after seeing the coffee that streamed out of the large, communal pot, I decided to treat myself at a nearby café. Besides, the box of donuts that sat next to the pot was already empty.

"Jim, good to see you this morning," Bull Durham bellowed at me as I entered the small café. He was seated at a two-person table next to the door. "If you're alone, why don't you join me?"

"Good morning, Bull. I have an appointment in a little bit down the street, but I can join you for a while." The odor of burnt toast wafted through the air.

"Ellen," Bull bellowed at the short woman behind the counter. "Bring Jim a cup of coffee, and how about if you bring us a few of those twists."

Ellen smiled, apparently used to Bull's bellowing. She came to our table a few seconds later carrying a fresh mug of coffee and a wicker basket containing four cinnamon twists. She had pulled her light brown hair back into a pony tail so tightly that it gave the illusion that the skin on her temples was being stretched backwards.

"Jim, this young lady here has been the apple of my eye ever since high school." He took hold of her wrist when he said this, and she didn't seem to mind. "She refused to marry me at least a dozen times. Married some sidewinder instead. Too much of a woman for him."

"Bull, be careful, or I'll be calling Torry again," Ellen said.

"Ha!" he laughed aloud. They both smiled.

I had no idea what was going on and couldn't help but wonder what Torry, Bull's wife, thought of his relationship with Ellen.

"Nice to meet you, Ellen."

"You're that guy, aren't you?" she asked.

"Yeah, Ellen, that's him, Tom's friend."

"Don't mind all of Bull's blubbering about me. He doesn't mean it. I have the unfortunate fate of being his only cousin."

"Jim," Bull said, "on a serious note. You were in Ms. Scott's SUV when it got struck by that bullet weren't you?"

"Yes," I tried to think if I mentioned that at lunch yesterday. "Neither one of us were hurt."

"Did you get a glimpse at who fired the shot?" he asked.

"No, wish I did. Why do you ask?"

"Oh, no reason really. My wife had a conversation with Brenda this morning. She mentioned something to her about having a conversation with that young man Poole and another guy. Someone had suggested that if you were hypnotized, you might remember seeing something."

"It's possible," I said. I hadn't really thought about it. "Usually though, that kind of hypnosis helps you focus on what you saw but can't fully describe. It's not all that effective in helping you remember things that didn't happen."

"You got me confused," Bull said.

"If I didn't see a person or a car, then hypnosis won't help me remember seeing them," I said.

"Guess that makes sense."

"How about Sylvia? Did she see anything?"

"No. She was driving," I said.

"That's too bad. Torry was all excited. Guess she watches too much TV."

Bull's curiosity got me thinking. I always wondered about people who asked too many questions concerning an ongoing investigation. Of course, that's like me calling the kettle black.

"Think they'll catch the guy?" he asked.

"I hope so."

"Me, too. I liked Wally."

"I know, you mentioned that yesterday. There are a lot of resources being thrown at this case. My guess is that the cops will have it wrapped up sooner rather than later," I said.

"I've lived here all my life and don't remember another series of killings like this one, Jim. I sure hope they solve it soon."

I had eaten one of the four cinnamon twists, and Bull had

two. I started to reach for the last one when Bull grabbed it. That clinched it. He would definitely get the honor of picking up the tab.

Ten minutes later, I reentered the police station hoping that Cat had returned. I thought this latest info from Glo could help bring the case to a quick resolution. At the minimum, I knew they would be very interested in it.

Chapter 13

"Why didn't you tell us this before?" Lieutenant Martin asked after I finished telling them what Glo had told me.

"I only learned--"

"And why are you interviewing our witnesses?" he interrupted me.

I leaned forward in my chair. I had enough of all this. "Marty, I've wanted to go home for several days now. I haven't sought out any witness. I didn't ask for the creep to take Frances from coffee shop while I was there, or to identify any of the dead bodies. The only reason Glo grabbed me to talk to was because she recognized me from my presence at the Miller's ranch. I didn't drive myself out there."

"Okay, okay, Cat, take this guy out of here and send him on his way."

She and I stood up and started for the door.

"Wait a second. Call Stephens and have him meet you two somewhere. Fill him in on all this. Seems to me, we need to be coordinating what we know with Austin. We should clue in the sheriff's office before we do so."

Cat and I walked down to her desk.

"He's had a rough morning. It's nothing to do with you, Jim."

"That's okay," I said without meaning it.

She dialed her phone and asked for Deputy Jerry Stephens. A moment later, she had him on the phone and gave him a ten-second version of the data I'd provided. She grunted an okay a couple of times and finished with a see you then.

"When do we get to see him?" I asked. I was ready to get this all behind me.

"He's actually not far from here right now. He'll meet us here in ten minutes," Cat said.

"Good."

"Let me get something clear," she said. "Why again did Glo tell you all this if she doesn't mind talking to us?"

"She doesn't want anyone to know that she's talking to the police. That's why she didn't come forward with everyone around yesterday at the sheriff's office. She was working up her courage to walk in to the police station yesterday when she saw me walk out. She has the good sense to be frightened by the people that did this to Frances and Wally. If you're discreet in your handling of her, I'm sure she'll be cooperative."

"We can be discreet," Cat said.

"I know. I told her so and even mentioned your name. I didn't provide Lieutenant Martin with her background, but she had a very rough one. Things have only gotten semi-normal for her in the past year," I said.

"I got that impression from what you did tell us. How bad did she have it?"

"I don't think it could've gotten much worse. I think she had already given up on herself. Then, one day, an older man took her off the streets."

"Oh, that sounds safe and normal," she said.

"She lucked out. She got the one-in-ten guy who wanted to rescue her, and who wasn't really a psycho."

"Sounds too good to be true."

"That's how she felt about it, too. I think she still does. Take it easy on her when you deal with her. Despite her claim that she's gotten her life straight, I think that she needs to be at the Miller's place for a lot longer. There is no other place she can go."

"Now it sounds like you want to take her home and protect her," she said.

I started to snap at her, but it dawned on me that she was correct. "I can't help but feel a need to protect her. I can't explain that, but I imagine in your line of work you've run across kids and young adults that you've felt a need to protect."

She nodded.

"But to clarify, I have no desire to take her home."

"I know," she said. "I have a bad habit of saying something I think might be witty before my brain engages. I shouldn't have said that. Do you think this guy who she says rescued her was the real deal?"

"For the most part, I think he was. Did he think if he took her home, fed her, gave her a safe place to stay, kept her warm and dry, and gave her access to a bath or shower, that she might reward him with sex? I'm sure that was in his mind from the beginning, too, but give him credit; he went about it in a very gentlemanly way."

"What single woman doesn't need her very own sugar daddy?" Cat asked.

"You serious?" I asked.

"Absolutely," she said, although I still wondered if she was pulling my leg.

"So, if I told you I was rich and could keep you in the style you'd prefer, you'd let me take you home?"

"Sorry, Charlie, we've already done a background check on

you. You ain't that rich." She at least said it with a smile.

"Hey," Cat said and stood up. "How are you today, Deputy Stephens?"

He had approached from behind me. I stood up and said hello.

"Jim, don't you think they should have you on their payroll for all you're doing for them?" Jerry said.

"Believe me, I'm keeping a tab," I said.

"Good luck with that," Cat said.

"So what do we have?" Jerry asked.

We huddled around Cat's desk, and I briefed Jerry on what I had learned from Glo. He interrupted me with a "Why didn't she tell us that?" a few times, but in the end I think he understood her concerns.

"The bottom line is that she did come forward. She wants you to have the information. She's just frightened," I said.

"Well, I for one would like to talk to her personally," Jerry said.

"I'm sure that she'll talk to you. Work something through Mrs. Miller, so you can get Glo away from the place under some pretext that can cover the fact she's talking to the cops. She trusts Bell, that's her name, right?" I said, and they nodded.

"The Lieutenant thinks we need to ask Austin to look into this. I suggest we go to them with a list of coordinated leads, you know, between the Sheriff and the Department here," Cat said.

"I agree," Jerry said. "Does he have some specific ideas?"

"I'm sure he does, but he asked me to coordinate with you. I think he wants you and me to develop the leads for Austin. You take the list back to have your boss okay them, and I'll do the same here. Any changes can be cleared by them before we send out a joint request."

"Sounds good, Cat."

They talked for a while listing the obvious. They didn't come up with many ideas, and some they mentioned likely had already been acted on by Austin. They both took notes. Cat wrote them down on paper, and Jerry typed them into a tablet. When they finished, Cat looked at me.

"Well, Jim, how'd we do?"

"Fine," I said, but there was one lead that they didn't think of, and it was nagging me too much to ignore. "One more you might want to pursue. Glo mentioned that she suspected Lunce may have had something to do with another girl's disappearance. The girl's name was Loretta. You can get more identification from the Millers. It might be interesting to see what the Austin PD or Travis County has on her."

"Good idea," Jerry said.

"I had thought about that when you mentioned her," Cat said. "It slipped my mind when we were working the leads. Thanks, Jim."

"And you just thought he was another pretty face, Cat," Jerry said.

"Not me, maybe Sylvia thinks that, huh Jim?" She said it to tease me, but she got more of a reaction out of Deputy Stephens.

"Who? Sylvia Scott? Is there something going on between you and her?" he asked me. He tried to keep his tone neutral, like he was playing along with Cat's picking on me. However, I could sense the surprise in his voice. Cat noticed it, too.

"Not really," I said. "I've been interested in the wine business and the real estate down here in this area. She's shown me around a little, and we've had dinner together, but I'm heading back to Clovis as soon as I can get away."

I caught Cat's eyes staring inquisitively at me. Jerry's eyes were also fixed on me.

"We've developed a good friendship," I continued. "She mentioned to me that you asked her out. Was that for Friday or Saturday night?"

"Friday."

"Well, don't tell her I told you, but she's really looking forward to it."

I could tell Cat wanted to jump into the conversation, and I didn't want her to. Luckily, Jerry had things to do and said he had to run. They agreed to coordinate the leads within their respective offices and with each other before sending them out. After he left, Cat turned to me.

"Okay, you're not getting out of here until you tell me what's going on."

I smiled at her. "Cat, there's really not much to tell. I'm a poor long-term prospect for Sylvia, and she knows it. Deputy Stephens is local, interested, and available.

"She couldn't put him off 'til you left town? Ouch."

I hadn't thought about it that way. "Come on, give us a break," I said.

She shook her head. "Love it," she said.

When I didn't respond, she looked down at her notes. "You want to stick around for a minute. I'm going to give Bell Miller a call and get Loretta's full ID. Then we can do a trace on her."

"Okay," I said.

The process only took a few seconds. "Well, how about that?"

"What do you have?" I asked.

"This poor kid Loretta was busted twice in Austin for prostitution this year," Cat said. "Sounds like your friend may have hit the nail on the head. I'm going to send this info to Deputy Stephens right now. Austin ought to be able to tell us what pimp controls Loretta, and that ought to lead us back to Lunce and his partners."

"That's great. Might not tell us who pulled the trigger, but it should really help in narrowing down the field," I said.

"It should. It might not be too easy though. You dealt much with prostitution?"

"Every time you ask me a question, Cat, I'm not sure what you're really asking. In this case, however, I can honestly say I have had little experience, no matter what you mean."

"Once they get broken into the profession, and I know that's a terrible way to put it, it's not unusual for the girl or guy to get traded. The pimp who's running her now may not have been involved with her procurement."

"But the cops over there ought to be able to work it back to the beginning, shouldn't they?" I asked.

"I think so. It may simply not be quick and easy."

"Got it. So what's my status?"

"Go home. We can deal with you on the phone. We've given you a hard time, but I appreciate your help."

I wanted to make a few phone calls before I left. I also needed lunch. My first call went to Sylvia. She answered and agreed to lunch. Still not being too familiar with Fredericksburg, I recommended we meet at her mom's place.

I called Tom and Brenda. She answered.

"Tom's out right now, Jim. How are you doing?"

"Fine. I wanted to call and thank you both for everything. I think you'll do great in the wine business."

"Thanks. We are both awfully happy you came down. And Jim?"

"Yes."

"I'm sorry you had to witness our fight over that bitch."

I knew right away to which bitch she referred. "I promise you, Brenda, that message from Lynn was a total shock to Tom."

"I know. I can read him like a book. His eyes would have given him away. I was just mad."

I wanted to ask her if she believed him, why she gave him such a hard time. "When I finish off the wine I bought from you, I'll be ordering more. By the way, Sylvia is quite optimistic that when people try it, they'll want more, too."

"I hope you and Sylvia have hit it off well," she said, although I thought she meant it more as a question.

"We have. She's a sweet girl."

"And Jim, did anyone ask you if you thought you might remember who shot Wally if you were hypnotized?"

"Yes, Bull asked me. You're quite the detective to think of it, Brenda, but it wouldn't do any good in this case."

"Oh, that's too bad, but I didn't think of it. Larry Poole asked about it. He wondered if either you or Sylvia might remember something more if you were hypnotized."

"No. We didn't see anything at all," I said.

I asked Brenda to relay my goodbyes to Tom and hung up.

Chapter 14

Sylvia was already at the restaurant when I arrived. She wore a light blue pullover sweater and a pair of jeans. Her hair looked a little different. I thought she had put a little wave in it, but it could have been the lighting in the room.

"You look very nice today," I said. I decided to play it safe and not comment on her hair.

"Thank you, Jim. So are they finally going to let you go home?"

"Looks like it," I said.

"I'm so happy that I got to know you, Jim. I'll miss you."

"Let's don't get all mushy, at least not before we eat."

Her mother came over to wait on us. She greeted me like an old friend. A scent of something frying wafted in from the kitchen. I ordered a BLT sandwich with some French fries. Sylvia stayed with a salad. We both ordered ice tea.

"Do you know a guy named Larry Poole?" I asked.

"No, I don't believe so. Why?"

"I don't know. Probably not important. I saw Deputy Stephens this morning."

"You did? Oh Jim, I feel so terrible about how I treated you."

"Don't be silly. He seems like a great guy. If it doesn't work out, I imagine I'll be back again someday." I didn't know why I said that, because I didn't have any specific plan to return. I liked the area, but unless the investigation forced me, I couldn't see a need to come back any time soon.

"Thanks, Jim. Are the police making any headway in their investigation?"

"I think so. My guess is that they'll have it wrapped up within a week."

"Oh, that'll be great," she said. "People around here are nervous and angry."

I didn't elaborate, and Sylvia didn't ask any more questions about the investigation. Our conversation went back to life in Fredericksburg and the growing wine business in the region.

"By the way, I got some good feedback from the Goat on Tom and Brenda's wine," she said after we had eaten most of our lunch.

"The Goat?" I asked.

"Yes. Remember the guy that called and wanted some free wine the other night?"

"Oh yeah, I remember."

"Well, he called me this morning to tell me everybody was happy with the wine. He also said that he would like to get some more, and by that I mean buy some more wine from the Broken Spur. He's going to carry it on his menu."

"That's good news. Do you ever get any calls by a customer saying a wine you sold them sucked?"

"Of course," she said. "I don't like those calls, but sometimes we get a bad batch, and sometimes the product simply isn't any good. I don't like getting those calls, but they happen."

"What's on your agenda for the rest of the day?" I asked.

"I was out on the road this morning. This afternoon I plan on locking myself in the office and getting orders filled. Unfortunately, I'll be there all day. I have a busy day ahead. How about you? When are you going home?"

"Hopefully, this afternoon no later than four. I almost feel that I should check in with Lieutenant Martin before I leave."

"Are you going to?" she asked.

"No. I almost feel that way." I said putting the emphasis on the word almost. "My compromise is to hang around for a couple hours more. I'm afraid if I go looking or asking, I'll be told to stick around another day."

"Wish I could spend some time with you, I really do, but you understand, don't you?" she said.

"You've got work. I understand," I said before it dawned on me that she could be saying something else. I didn't follow up on the topic. After another five minutes, we said our goodbyes, accompanied with an awkward hug.

I got back in my car wondering where to go next when my phone rang. I answered, and Officer Cat Morris spoke to me.

"Guess what?" she said.

"What?"

"Loretta's no longer in Austin."

"That was quick," I said.

"We didn't get it from Austin. I ran a different search and came up with a recent hit down in the Eagle Ford area south of San Antonio."

"Eagle Ford? Is that a town?" I asked.

"It's an area where they're doing a hell of a lot of drilling right now for oil, shale oil. It's like the Wild West down there. Boom towns built out of trailers, and money flowing more freely than water."

"What's she doing there?"

"Probably the same thing, prostitution. She hasn't been busted down there, but she came up as a person of interest in a large theft. There's enough data on record to make me pretty sure it's the same woman. Won't be hard to verify it."

"It would be good to have her interviewed," I said.

"That's the game plan. I'm heading down there in a little while, so I wanted to tell you again thanks for your help. Have a safe trip home. Give me a call in a few days, and I'll update you on what's going on."

"I appreciate that, Cat. Tell me though, how did you wrangle the trip south to interview her?"

"The guys down there are swamped. They didn't have the infrastructure to handle the sudden population growth, and they've been playing catch up ever since. They said they could locate her, but suggested we send someone down to do the interview."

"Well, that worked out. How long of a drive is it?"

"We should be able to get there in three hours. Hopefully, we'll get to interview her tonight," she said.

"Any way you can bring her back with you as a material witness?"

"We hadn't planned on doing that."

"It might help her break away from the group that's controlling her," I said.

"I'll suggest that to the Lieutenant. It might be a good idea. We wouldn't have to try to find her again if we need her."

"That's right, and they may try to hide her once they get wind of what you're doing?"

"Good point. I've got to go. You take care of yourself, Jim."

"You, too, Cat."

I hung up. It would be good if they could do something to help Loretta. At this point it could be too late, but I hoped not. In the Air Force, I had never been involved in the investigation of prostitution. It had been around but always off base. Prostitution was one of those matters the local authorities handled.

Not all male and female prostitutes were forced into their profession. I knew that, but I also believed a sizeable proportion had been forced into it. Loretta didn't leave the Millers' ranch because she wanted to become a prostitute. I believed what Glo believed. She was forced into it by a monster named Benjamin Lunce and his associates. With any luck, in a few days a number of those thugs would be off the streets.

I drove to the La Quinta, packed up, and checked out. After contemplating whether or not to leave early despite my comment about staying until four, I started my car and pointed it west. I hadn't traveled a hundred yards when my phone rang again. I pulled into a gas station parking lot to take the call.

"Tom, what can I do for you?"

"Brenda said you called. Sorry I wasn't here."

"That's okay. I just wanted to say goodbye. I'm heading home in a few minutes."

"I wanted to give you another bottle. This is a blend we're experimenting with. It's not for sale yet, but I'd love for you to take some home and let me know what you think."

"Something for me to drink on the road," I joked.

"Don't even say that. I'll be happy to bring it into town. Save you the trip out here."

"No reason for you to do that. I'm in my car right now. It'll only take me twenty minutes or so to be at your place."

He agreed. I made a u-turn and headed east. I didn't actually want the bottle of wine, but taking it was less painful than telling Tom I didn't want any more of his wine. As I turned off the highway onto the small road that led to Tom's vineyard, I saw a small figure standing in the trees close to where Tom had discovered Frances' body. My curiosity got the better of me, and I parked my car next to an old jeep.

I recognized the person right away. "Hi, Bell. Are you okay?"

"Yes," she said, but I could tell she'd been crying. "This is the spot right?"

"Yes. They found her right over there." I pointed a few yards to her right.

"Such a waste. You never knew her, did you?"

"No."

"She was a sweet girl. A little pixie, full of life and innocence. She had taken a break from college. Maybe that's what made him feel like she was vulnerable."

I didn't know what to say. I stood there staring at the ground.

"She was so nice. Despite her claim that she needed a break from college, she seemed so happy with her life. She couldn't wait to marry Wally. Her father was supposed to come down at the end of the month to meet him and his parents. Now he's come to take her body home." A few tears fell, and Bell dabbed a handkerchief at her eyes.

"Did Glo talk to you?" I asked.

"Yes. Were you the one she spoke to?"

"I talked to her."

"But you're not the police?" she asked.

"No."

"Glo, she's the miracle among us."

"Miracle?"

"She told you her background?"

"Yes," I said.

"To survive that and become a normal, no, more than normal, to become a really good person has to be a miracle. You know, she didn't just have a bad event in her life. Her entire life, up to about two years ago was a terrible event. I can't imagine how a person can absorb all that happened to her and still turn out normal."

"She seems to have adjusted well."

"She had trouble sleeping when she first arrived. She told me her story when she came. She wanted to make sure I was okay with her in the house." She laughed softly. "I told her we've housed ex-cons before, so we could probably handle her. She let me know she had spent plenty of time in juvenile detention and even a number of nights in jail. Those were some of the better days in her life."

"Has her sleeping gotten better?" I asked.

"Oh yeah, I forgot what I was going to say. About two weeks after she joined us, I bought her a big stuffed bear. I named it Allister and gave it to her. That did the job. We all need a security blanket of some sort."

"You're a good woman, Mrs. Miller."

"We try. All we can do is try."

"Glo is very happy she's at the ranch. I think she sees it as a way to further transition into real life."

"I'm sad to say she's seen more of real life than we have. I just hope we can continue to help her adjust to a normal life," she said.

"I better head to the Hasbens' house up the road. They're waiting for me. You take care of yourself, Bell, and tell Glo I said hello."

"You think the killings will continue?" she asked.

"Hope not."

"Me, too. When I was a little girl, two families got into a feud. I think this has me as scared as I was back then."

I had no solution for her. "It will be over soon. The police have a lot of leads."

"I pray it will end soon. The innocent have always been easy prey for the evil ones."

I thought I saw her shiver.

"Can I get you anything? You look cold."

"I'm not cold. I just can't stop thinking about how afraid she must have been."

"Did you talk to her before she left?" I asked.

"No. I saw her briefly that morning. She had a look in her eyes that made me think she might have been crying, but there was more to it than that. I was busy with my own chores, so I didn't say anything to her. I remember thinking that I could talk to her later."

"That's a normal reaction. You had no way of foreseeing what was going to happen," I said.

"I tell myself that. Yet my mind keeps telling me now that it was fear in her eyes that I saw, not tears. I had a terrible dream last night. Maybe she wanted to talk to me, but I just rushed on with my chores. Maybe I could've done something."

"I had the same dream," I said.

She looked at me, not understanding.

"I stood next to her in coffee shop that morning. I stood there and did nothing while she was dragged out of the little cafe by her hair."

"The man had a gun and shot someone. I heard that on the

news. What could you have done?"

"That's what I try to tell myself, but my dreams won't let it go."

"You're being unfair to yourself," she said.

"As are you," I said. "In hindsight, we can always wish we had done something different, but it does no good to tear ourselves down. Believe me, I know."

"I guess I do, too." She reached out and grabbed my hand for a second before letting go.

I left her and drove the short distance to Tom's house. Brenda met me at the door.

"Come on in for a minute, Jim. I know you're in a hurry to go. Tom's got a bottle of wine for you, and I've got some freshly baked cookies."

"Cookies? You shouldn't have."

"If I remember right, Jim, you've always been a sucker for baked goods."

She had it right. I stayed for about ten minutes before I left with a bottle of wine and a dozen cookies in a zip-lock bag. I didn't think the cookies would last to the New Mexico border.

Brenda hadn't mentioned Lynn one time and had even been cordial to Tom. She appeared to be over the whole video thing, but I doubted it. I wondered what would happen the next time she and Lynn bumped into each other.

The gas gauge indicated the Mustang had less than a half of tank left, so I turned into a gas station a few miles east of Fredericksburg. I had a long drive ahead of me. I finished pumping the gas into my car and watched a red pickup truck pull up to the store front. Cappy jumped out of the truck and rushed into the station.

I debated what to do. I knew that Larry Poole said that he saw Lunce, Frances, and a black man driving toward Austin. However, I also knew that thinking Cappy was that black man was based on nothing more than that he was the only black man I had met in Fredericksburg. For me to think Poole saw him in the vehicle with Frances the day she disappeared might be the height of profiling. I almost felt stupid even wanting to talk to him. Plus, there was something about Poole that troubled me.

A number of other questions popped into my mind as I left the Mustang at the pump and walked toward the store. Why did Cappy seem to be in a hurry? Had the police already talked to him? How direct should I be in approaching him?

At first, I didn't see him in the store. I grabbed a small bag of chips and strolled down an aisle. The reason for Cappy's urgency to get into the store became obvious when I saw him come out of the men's room. He resolved my concerns regarding how to approach him by walking right up to me.

"Hey, you're our trespasser aren't you?" he said with a smile.

"Yeah, Jim West." I extended my hand.

He took it. "That's right. Call me Hank. We meet in better circumstances."

"For sure. Did the police ever get back with you on the shooting?"

"No, I haven't heard a thing."

"So they haven't talked to you?" I asked.

"No. Why should they?" his smile faded a little.

"Oh, I'm sorry. They've talked to me a dozen times in the last few days. I thought maybe we could share some inside info."

"Wish they had. I have a lot of questions, but I'm afraid I couldn't help them much even if they did want to talk to me."

"I think they're making progress," I said.

"I hope so. Wally was a great guy."

"Did you know Benjamin Lunce? He was the guy who kidnapped the female victim, and then later someone killed him?"

"No, I didn't know him. Why?" he asked.

"I think the police are digging into his background. Even though he was dead when the third murder took place, he seems to be at the heart of all this."

"Where did he work?"

"Different places, I think. He worked on engines, both tractor engines and truck engines. I heard he worked for a company in San Marcos, but he also did a lot of part-time work up here," I said. My comments didn't appear to register with him. "In addition to his legitimate activities, I suspect he was a pretty bad guy."

"I hate all this stuff going down here in this area. It's really a peaceful place. I thought I left all this killing behind overseas." He shook his head to emphasize his point.

"Former military?"

"Yes, Army Ranger."

I could see the pride in his eyes.

"What brought you here?"

"I grew up in San Antonio, and my family spent a lot of time up here as a kid. I went to A&M with the idea of becoming a vet. Somewhere along the line I got patriotic, joined the Corps, and the next thing I knew I was an officer in the Army."

"Good for you."

"Mr. Rondit's son was my best friend over there. He lost both legs in an explosion. I came back here a couple years ago with him. I promised him that I would help his Dad until he could step in and take over."

"How's he doing?" I asked.

"Actually very good. It's a slow process, but he's ahead of schedule."

"Very nice of you doing that for them."

"I'm learning a lot. I still plan on becoming a vet. The time on the ranch will help me, because I plan on specializing in the larger animals, not house pets."

"Interesting. I wish you the best," I said. I meant it, too. "By the way, do you know Larry Poole?"

"I've met him briefly. He's helped out on the ranch a couple of times, but I don't know him. Never been out drinking or hanging with him. Why do you ask?"

"Don't know for sure myself."

We said our goodbyes, and I left feeling a little stupid for my suspicions. If I had to guess, Hank separated from the military when he held the rank of captain, and Cappy was a private nickname reserved only for the Rondit family.

I entered Fredericksburg city limits at the same time as I saw Sylvia's Expedition heading out of town. I waved as I went by, but she stared straight ahead. As she passed me, the hairs on the back of my neck went crazy. A man sat next to her in the car. I only caught a glimpse of him since my attention had been focused at Sylvia. However, something about him also nagged at the back of my mind. I couldn't nail it down.

One thing I did know for certain: I didn't like the look on Sylvia's face. She looked like she might have been crying.

I hit my brakes more out of instinct than logic. As soon as I could, I turned the Mustang around and headed back east. With all this back and forth driving, if my car could speak, it would likely be screaming at me to pick a direction and stick to it.

Hadn't Sylvia told me that she had to stay in the office for the rest of the day? She said something about spending the afternoon filling orders, that she had a busy day ahead. Of course, that may have just been an easy way to get rid of me.

I couldn't see the Expedition, so I accelerated above the speed limit. My contacts with law enforcement here had to be enough to get a ticket expunged. I called Sylvia's phone hoping to get some reassurance. The call went unanswered. There could be a hundred logical explanations for her driving out of town. Yet nothing felt right. I wished that I had taken a better look at the man in the car with her. I felt like he was someone I had met, but who? What was going on?

I pressed further down on the accelerator.

Chapter 15

"Hello?" A man answered my second attempt to contact Sylvia by phone.

"May I speak to Sylvia?" I asked.

"Sorry, she doesn't appear to be here right now."

"This is her cell phone I reached, right?"

"Yes it is. I'm Trey, I work for Ms. Scott. Want me to give her a message?"

"Tell her Jim West called and have her give me a call. Is it common for her to leave her phone behind?"

"No. She'll be mad at herself," Trey said.

"I kind of wanted to see her before I left," I said. "Do you know where she might have gone?"

"I didn't think she was going anywhere this afternoon. Are you her friend from New Mexico?"

"Yes. I helped her the other night when the place was getting broken into."

I thought I heard a short laugh at the other end. I didn't need any more wisecracks about Sylvia rescuing me.

"Trey, I thought I saw her driving out of town with some guy a minute ago. That's why I called."

"Certainly she has the right to hang around with some other guy, Mr. West," his voice almost sounded condescending.

"That's not what I mean. Did she expect any visitors today at the office? I think she might be in danger."

"Danger? That's crazy. Why?"

"I don't know," I said. "I thought I saw one of those large desktop monthly calendars on her desk. Can you look at it and let me know if there's anything jotted down for today."

The phone remained silent for about fifteen seconds. "Sorry sir, nothing in today's square but a scribbled JW with the word lunch. I think that might have been you."

"It was. Thanks, Trey. I may be concerned about nothing, but have her call me."

"Will do, but I'm sure she's okay," he said.

I found myself trapped behind two large trucks. Before I closed in on them, I thought I caught a glimpse of the Expedition far ahead. Trailing close behind the trucks, I couldn't see anything and knew I would be losing ground. Highway 290 had four lanes. I figured the two trucks wouldn't be racing each other at five miles per hour below the speed limit forever.

I backed off a little and slid the car over to the right shoulder. It had plenty of smooth pavement which allowed me to get a look ahead. I saw that the Expedition had turned off 290 and headed south. The truck driver in front of me moved over a few feet onto the shoulder. He must have thought I intended to pass him on the right and didn't like the idea. I moved the Mustang back onto the driving lane behind him.

The turnoff seemed to take forever to reach. When I reached it, the Expedition had disappeared. I thought I recognized the road as the one I had been on a day or to earlier with Sylvia. I sped up, but the turns in the road forced me to slow back down. I reached a V in the road and went right without slowing. I passed a sign that told me I was approaching Luckenbach. Shooting past an entrance to a large parking lot to my right, I noticed a handful of cars parked in the distance. I slowed down and made a sharp turn into a second entrance.

One spin through the parking lot and I knew they hadn't

come in here. The Expedition would've stood out in this open expanse. The huge lot seemed out of proportion, too large for the handful of old buildings. I noticed one of the buildings had a sign identifying it as a dance hall. I guessed that when they had events here, large crowds could show up despite its being miles from anywhere. After all, there was that song.

At least I could now say that I'd been there. It would rank up there with the time I stood on a corner in Winslow, Arizona.

I stopped at the exit and debated which way I should go. The Expedition could be anywhere by now. I had no real evidence to make me think Sylvia was in any danger. Maybe the guy in the Expedition was one of her employees. I tried to tell myself I had overreacted, but my gut knotted up and just wouldn't listen.

Sylvia had driven me out in this direction the day Wally was murdered. I remembered we went to the old lady's place. I couldn't recall her name or the name of her vineyard, but I thought I remembered how we got there.

I steered the Mustang back the way I had come, and at the now inverted V in the road, turned right. I kept to the speed limit. I couldn't see hurrying now, since I had no idea where they were. The vineyard was a long shot. I turned onto what I thought was the dirt driveway. About twenty yards off the road, I came to a locked gate. I backed out realizing I had turned too early. I drove another half mile before I recognized the entrance and saw the sign to the Royal Ridge Vineyards.

The Expedition stood out like a big, blue boat in a sea of beiges and browns. I hit the brakes. Sylvia had parked the Expedition right in front of the main house. I didn't see anyone. All of a sudden, I felt kind of foolish. No one would have brought her out here to harm her. Why bring her to a place where there were other witnesses?

My Mustang crept in close to the Expedition, while I tried to decide whether to stay or leave. I stopped the car and took the keys out of the ignition. I climbed out of the car thinking I might as well say hello since I was already here. I would look pretty stupid if I simply drove away. However, no one appeared to notice my arrival.

The sun heated the mostly still air. I didn't see or hear anyone. In fact, everything seemed too quiet. I walked over and checked out the empty Expedition. I heard a noise that startled me more than it should have. I jerked my head around and noticed the front door of the house was open a few inches. The sound I heard came from the door creaking as it moved a little one way or the other in the soft breeze.

"Hello?" I said. No one replied. The hairs on the back of my neck resumed their effort to dance away. My hand involuntarily reached back and tried to rub them into submission. I walked up to the front door and pushed it the rest of the way open. "Hello," I said again. I couldn't remember the old woman's name. "Sylvia?"

The furniture looked old like its owner. The area rug that covered most of the wooden flooring in the large room just off the foyer had a well-worn trail where people had walked from the entry through the room to the kitchen. The red and green pattern on the rug had faded almost completely away. A large overstuffed green sofa sat against a far wall. A few patterned Queen Anne chairs and a coffee table filled out the room. Despite appearing old and used, the room looked clean and recently dusted.

I walked through to the kitchen. Like the larger living room, the kitchen could have used a remodeling, but the counters and floor appeared clean and uncluttered. I looked out the kitchen window at a couple of large buildings but saw no one.

Texas is not a state where one should go exploring someone else's house without an invitation. The law allows a homeowner to shoot first and ask questions later. I knew this and therefore wondered if I should leave the house or continue looking around. I peeked in the downstairs bathroom and the closets while I considered my options.

Not feeling too confident with my decision, I headed upstairs. "Hello, anyone home?" I called out again. "I don't mean you any harm. I found the front door open. I just want to make sure everyone is okay." I felt kind of foolish talking to an empty house, but I deemed it a better choice than surprising someone who might be holding a shotgun pointed my way.

The upstairs turned out as empty as the downstairs. Only one of the three bedrooms appeared to have been used recently. It also had a flowery odor that I imagined came from one of those plug-in air fresheners. A small room at the end of the upstairs hallway must have had thirty pictures of children and young adults in it. In several, the pictures included the woman who owned this house.

I wondered where everyone was and remembered Sylvia mentioning that the woman operated a bar or a pub somewhere on the property. That had to be where they were. I hurried downstairs and went out front. I left the door ajar like I found it. A smaller, wooden building stood to my right next to the circular drive in front of the house. I hadn't paid much attention to it on my arrival, because it looked dark and empty.

As I approached the building, I noticed a closed sign on the door. Next to it, a second note said the place hoped to open in the spring. I looked in a window. Like the house, the place looked neat and clean. Chairs were stacked on top of the tables.

I didn't like any of this. The other day, Sylvia had taken the dirt road off the driveway that went around and behind the house. She'd parked in front of an outbuilding where the cases of wine had been stored. I walked the same dirt trail the fifty yards to the building. Other than a few birds twittering and a lizard scampering ahead of me, I saw and heard nothing during the walk. The front door to the building was locked. I tried unsuccessfully to lift the garage-type door. I walked around the building and found the back door locked, too.

Another thirty yards to my right stood a larger building that housed the machinery and equipment used to make and age the wine. I had seen a building like it at Tom's place. He referred to it as the winery. I went to it. My pace became a little quicker. The building appeared to be secured until I found a side window that had been overlooked. Someone left it open about an inch. It didn't make sense that Sylvia would've entered through the window. However, the guy could've gone in through a door, done something to her inside, and left by a window after locking the door from the inside.

My imagination toyed with me. I did my best to ignore it, although I had convinced myself by now something was not right. I pushed the window up and climbed inside. A muffled noise came from somewhere on the far side of the building. Creeping around two large wine presses, I considered dialing 911. What would I tell them? I had suspicions, but no real evidence that any crime had been or was going to be committed.

The sound I heard stopped. The metal building gave off an occasional creak or popping sound that I contributed to the sun's heat or the light breeze. A cloud must have moved in front of the sun, as the light coming in through the windows dimmed. For a second, I thought about looking for a light switch. I had called out in the house without hesitation, but my mood had changed. For whatever reason, I now felt that I shouldn't advertise my presence.

I walked as quietly as I could. Two large sinks hung against the wall to my right, and a large, green hose half hung on a nearby holder. The rest of the hose meandered on the concrete floor in front of the sinks. A small puddle of water covered an area of the floor next to the hose. Not wanting to, I peered into the oversized sinks. While I didn't fully understand my fear of finding something horrendous in the sinks, I breathed a sigh of relief after discovering them empty.

I remembered my encounter with the burglar at Sylvia's warehouse. He had surprised me when I was doing much the same thing I was doing now. No way I'd be tricked again, I said to myself.

A bee or wasp flew by my ear, and I instinctively swatted at it. I realized then that I had to relax. My adrenalin had already kicked in. I leaned against some shelving that held hundreds of empty bottles. I steadied my breathing and tried to listen for any sounds. I heard nothing suspicious. After about thirty seconds, I continued my search of the building. I found it as empty as the house. I tried to figure out what had made the sound and had given up, when it suddenly started again.

One of the large vats that processed the grape juice into wine was on. Periodically, it did whatever it was supposed to do and made a muffled noise when it did. At least recognizing from where the sound had come lowered my stress level. I began to wonder if Sylvia and whoever she had in her SUV with her may have left the Expedition here and driven off with someone else. That would make sense. I went outside and despite my anxiety, had made up my mind to leave.

I took a couple steps toward the front of the house and my car when I heard the sound of metal striking something hard. I started to call out her name, but an impulse prevented me from doing so. For whatever reason, the sharp sound seemed ominous. More than before, I felt like something had to be wrong. I stood there, looked hard in the direction of the sound, and listened.

The sound came from the side of the property. It didn't repeat itself, but the sound had been distinct. Someone was digging nearby. A shovel or a pick ax had struck rock. I studied the area around the buildings and sheds. The immediate area had little to no vegetation. Immediately behind the buildings, rows of grapes stretched for a few hundred yards. Off to the side, some forty to fifty yards from the buildings and in the direction from which the sound had come, the terrain had a more natural look. Scattered tall trees and a lot of thick underbrush and smaller trees blocked my view beyond a couple of yards into the undergrowth.

Listening as I walked the fifty yards to the bushes, I didn't hear any more sounds of digging. I discovered a path that provided safe passage through the underbrush from the thorn bushes and cactus. I followed the path as it wound through about twenty yards of surprisingly thick vegetation. It opened up to a clearing that contained a small pond. Only then did I see what had made the noise. A chill ran through me.

Chapter 16

Not thirty yards from where I stood, a man with a shovel was digging a large hole at the edge of the pond. I only had a view of his back, so I didn't recognize him. Next to him a body lay on the ground. Despite her back also being to me, I recognized the clothing Sylvia had worn at lunch. I forced myself to stay still and evaluate the situation. Every fiber in me wanted to charge the man, screaming as I did.

Instead, I knelt down and considered my options. The terrain had a drop of about four feet half way between the man and me. The path wound around the drop off and had a more gradual slope, but taking it added an additional ten or fifteen yards to reach him. I didn't see anything to use for cover once I left the edge of the bushes. I felt certain the guy wouldn't hear me coming until I jumped off the ledge and landed a few yards short of him. He might not hear me at all if I stuck to the path, but that would put me out in the open for several additional seconds. Although I didn't see a weapon other than the shovel, I felt certain he had one. I couldn't see him forcing Sylvia out of her office without one.

I didn't have a weapon. I saw a rock the size of a baseball doing nothing next to my feet and decided to give its existence a purpose. I picked it up, took a deep breath, and sprinted at the man.

My plan worked pretty much as expected. He didn't hear me until I landed from my running leap off the ledge. He turned and looked at me in surprise. Rather than simply swing the shovel at me, which could have been lethal since I couldn't have stopped my forward progress at that point, he reached for the pistol he had tucked into his belt. I threw the rock at him from about five yards. I should've thrown it at his center of mass, but his face and eyes staring at me were irresistible.

He ducked and the rock grazed his left ear. Although the rock only did minimal damage, it did disrupt his attempt to draw his weapon. As a result, I collided with Larry Poole at full speed. My momentum carried us both into the shallow pond.

We rolled around for what seemed to me to be an eternity. At first, I tried desperately to prevent him from getting to his pistol while he tried to grab it from his belt. He pulled away from me and stood up. We both realized at that point that the weapon had fallen out. He started to run for the shore. I didn't know if he had seen the pistol or wanted to get to the shovel, but I leapt and tackled him. We both thrashed around in the water some more.

Poole had youth and energy on his side. Our strength seemed evenly matched. I had to rely on my experience and knowledge of fighting. I attacked any and all the vulnerable points of the body that got exposed and in range. I struck at his throat, his temples, eyes, knees, groin, etc. He kept trying to slam his fists into my face. Neither of us could get leverage in the muddy water. More than once, one of us would go for a choke hold only to have the other slip out.

My break came when we both tumbled against the shoreline. He fell and sprawled face down to my left only inches away. I fell to knees and hands, and my right hand landed on a rock a little bigger than the one I had first thrown at him. Without much thought, I lifted the rock and smashed it into the back of

Poole's head as he began to get up. He collapsed back against the bank. Not having much confidence in my off-balance effort and feeling zero pity for the guy, I struck him a second time. He didn't move again. I rolled him over. I couldn't tell if he was unconscious or dead.

I stood up, and a wave of dizziness spread over me. I went down on one knee and attempted to control my breathing. It only took about fifteen seconds before I felt better. Standing up, I looked over at Sylvia's crumpled body. I figured Poole had already killed her, but I went to check her to be sure. She lay on her side with her arm across her face. I slid her arm back to her side and gently lifted her head. She surprised me by attempting to say something. It came out as a soft murmur, but the sound was distinct enough to reassure me it wasn't just an escape of trapped air.

"Sylvia," I said. "Wake up, Sylvia."

Her eyes flickered, but then she was out again. I felt for a pulse and found a weak one. I reached for my cell phone. When I saw it, I knew the pond water had ruined it. It dripped a green liquid and looked dead. I tried to dial 911 anyway. Nothing happened. I looked around in hopes I could see something that might help.

Poole groaned and started to move. I rushed over to him. He appeared to have relapsed into unconsciousness. I removed my leather belt and did my best to fasten his hands together behind his back. Unless it's flexible, a belt is not the best thing with which to tie a person's hands. I didn't have a lot of confidence mine would hold him, but it would have to do.

I looked back at Sylvia. She had propped herself up on one elbow and looked at me. Her eyes seemed to have a hard time focusing. Her mouth opened, but the sound that came out didn't make sense. I returned to her and helped her into a sitting position. For the first time, I had a good view of the wound to her head. It looked nasty. I wondered if Poole had hit her from behind with the shovel. Blood and mud were matted in her hair, and she had a large lump that looked a little scary. She also had a minor bruise on her left cheek.

"You're going to be okay, Sylvia. Just take it easy."

She looked at me while I spoke but made no effort to respond. I couldn't tell if she understood me or not.

"It's going to be okay," I kept saying. I sat next to her and rocked her in my arms. I faced Poole while I held Sylvia. Although I had no idea how I was going to get Sylvia to safety and a hospital, and at the same time turn Poole over to the police, I was determined to do both.

I scanned the ground around us looking for Poole's phone and the pistol. I didn't see either. If he had a phone, and it had remained in his pocket during our fight, it would have the same water damage mine had. Still, I thought it couldn't hurt to check his pockets.

"No, I can sit," Sylvia said in a weak voice when I started to lay her back down.

"What? Is that all you can say? No how nice it is to see you again, Jim?" I said grinning. I wanted her to relax as much as possible.

She looked at me with a look that appeared confused, but a small smile tried to make an appearance on her face.

"I'm just going over there to see what he has in his pockets," I said.

She looked over at Poole. Suddenly, she grabbed my arm,

and I heard her take a sharp breath.

"It's okay. He's not going to be able to hurt you again. He's tied up."

"My head," she moaned and reached for the nasty lump on the back of her head.

I stopped her hand and held onto it for a minute. "Sylvia, look at me."

She did.

"Do you know who I am?"

"Jim."

"Good. You're going to be okay. You have a nasty bruise on your head. It's been bleeding but appears to have stopped." I let go of her hand.

She reached to the back of her head and felt her wound. She grimaced.

"Do you remember how you got here or where you are?" I asked.

She looked at me. I could tell she was trying to piece it all together.

"While you're trying to remember, I need to go check his pockets. Okay?"

"Okay."

Poole had a wallet in his back pocket and his phone in his front right pocket. The wet phone didn't work. I hung onto his wallet. He appeared to be regaining consciousness, too. I picked up the shovel. It would serve to get Poole's attention if he became obstinate.

I wondered what role he had played in all the killings, or if this had been some bizarre stand-alone crime. Sylvia started making gagging sounds like she was throwing up. She had turned her head away from me. She bent her head close to the ground. I returned to her side. My mind went back to trying to resolve our current dilemma. I needed to get both Poole and Sylvia to the house. I might be able to use the phone there to call for help, but getting them there would be difficult. I didn't want to leave either of them alone.

Sylvia, at a minimum, had a concussion and needed medical attention. I didn't think Poole's injuries were significant, but even if they were, I didn't feel the urgency to get him to a doctor. I ached all over, but I knew I only needed a shower.

"Can you walk?"

"In a minute," Sylvia said without looking up at me.

I needed Sylvia to be able to walk on her own. That way I could drag Poole if he didn't want to cooperate. While I waited for Sylvia to try to stand up, I wondered how much trouble I might get into if I broke both of Poole's legs with the shovel and left him here until the police showed up to retrieve him.

"I'm awful dizzy," Sylvia said.

"That's okay. We're in no hurry," I lied. We needed to get this thing over with as soon as possible. "Do you remember coming out here?"

She pushed herself back into a sitting position. "He came to the office. I'm not sure of the time. At first, he just talked about the wine business. I guess once he was certain there was no one else there, he pulled out a gun and told me he would kill me if I didn't do exactly what he said. I started to argue with him, but he hit me." Her hand went instinctively to the bruise on her cheek.

"Did he say what he wanted with you?" I asked.

"No. I thought he wanted to rob me. When he told me he

wanted me to drive him somewhere, all I could think of was that he was going to take me somewhere and rape me. I was terrified." She stopped talking and looked at her hands. I waited for her to start up again. "When he had me bring him here, I didn't know what was going to happen. I knew Bee had a heart attack yesterday and had been taken to the hospital."

"The woman who owns this place?" I asked.

"Yes. She should be okay. Expects to be back in a week or so. She told the few people who work part time for her to consider it vacation time. I think he," Sylvia nodded her head at Poole, "is one of the guys that work here once in a while. He told me when we arrived that no one would be here to bother us. He called around for a minute or two and double checked the house, but like he said, no one was here."

"Did he say why he brought you out here?"

"He said he was worried I might have seen something that I shouldn't have."

"Did he say what?" I asked.

"No, but when I tried to convince him that I didn't see anything and asked him to let me go, he said that he would make it quick and easy for me. Then he said something like 'not like her'."

"Who did he mean by that?"

"I think he must have been talking about the young woman who had been killed. I didn't ask him who. I was too afraid. We walked out of the house, and that's about all I remember. I vaguely remember seeing the pond, but I'm not sure," Sylvia said. "Help me stand up."

I grabbed her elbows and lifted her. She appeared unsteady, but she managed to stand there and looked around.

"Who dug the hole?" she asked.

"He did. I think he intended to bury you there."

"What?" she gripped my arm and held on to it for extra balance.

"You're safe now. We need to get to a phone to call 911. Don't worry, I won't let him do anything else to you," I said.

"Didn't you bring your phone?" she asked.

"It got soaked just like me when I tried to convince Poole to surrender. It's dead. So is his. Your phone is back in the office. Once you feel up to it, I'll need you to go back to the house and use the phone there to call for some help."

"Are you sure that you'll be safe here with him if he comes to?"

"I think so, but keep an eye on him for a second. I want to look for his pistol. Just shout if he moves at all. I'll be real close." I kept the shovel and walked the few steps to the edge of the water. The pond water looked like it never got very clear, and our rolling around and fighting in it made it opaque. The pistol could've been sitting in two inches of water, and I wouldn't have been able to see it.

"No use," I said when I returned to Sylvia's side. "The water's too dirty to see anything. Think you're steady enough to walk to the house?"

"I think so. It's not far. Want me to wait at the house or come back here after I call?"

I started to answer, when our plan for a quick and safe conclusion to our predicament came to an abrupt end.

"Poole! Poole! Where are you man?" A man shouted from somewhere near the main house.

"Hey Poole!" A second man called out.

"I'm down here!" Poole tried to shout a reply. His voice came out hoarse and raspy. He had regained consciousness at some point. He tried to get to his feet.

I took four quick steps and swung the shovel about the same time Poole tried to shout again. The back side of the blade smacked against the side of his head, and Poole fell in a heap to the ground next to the hole. Some small part of me again wondered if I had killed him. I yanked my shirt off, rolled it as fast as I could, and tied it around his head covering his mouth. I pushed his limp body into the hole. He landed face down in an awkward position.

"Did you kill him?" Sylvia asked. She looked frightened again.

"I doubt if we were that lucky. Give me a hand to spread some of this dirt over him. I don't think someone can see into this hole from up there." I looked up to the spot where the path came out of the bushes by the small ledge. "To be safe though, I'd like to get a little dirt in there over his clothing to help camouflage anything they might see."

We worked quickly. I used the shovel and Sylvia scooped the loose dirt out of the pile with her hands.

"Poole! Where are you?" The man sounded closer and angrier.

"Time's up," I said in a whisper to Sylvia. "Come with me."

I didn't take a chance on her not following me. I grabbed her hand and pulled her along behind me as I ran toward a spot under the ledge where some bushes grew out of it and along its base. We made it to the spot without being seen. We crouched quietly as close as we could against the rock face of the ledge. The bushes gave us adequate cover and the rock ledge here was about five feet high. We would be easily discovered by anyone who went out to the pond and looked our way, but from the three other directions it would be hard to spot us.

"Poole!" one of the men shouted again. He sounded close. I hoped the impromptu gag did its job if Poole came to.

"Do you see him anywhere?" the second man shouted from further away.

"No. I thought I heard something from over here, but I don't see him."

"I'll call his phone again," the second man said. He sounded a little closer than before.

Chapter 17

Sylvia grabbed my arm. I turned and held my finger to my lips. She shook her head and pointed to the ground about twenty feet from where we cowered against the side of the ledge. On the other side of cactus plant, a large rattlesnake seemed content and coiled in the warm sun. I looked at Sylvia, rolled my eyes, and shook my head. What else could go wrong today?

I heard one of the men say something, but he seemed further away than before and didn't shout. The other man said something, and then one of them shouted out Poole's name again.

"Think they're gone?" Sylvia asked about a minute later.

"I don't know. Did Poole say anything about meeting anyone else here?"

"Not to me," she said.

"I guess he planned on leaving your car here. These two must have come to drive him away. I assume they knew what he was doing here. That makes them dangerous, too."

"What did Poole think I saw?"

"My guess is that he thinks you may have seen him when he shot at Wally and hit your car," I said.

"You're kidding. I didn't see anything."

"I know. I didn't either. He's seen too much TV. He's worried that if we were hypnotized, we might remember seeing him."

"What?" she asked.

"Don't worry, if our luck holds we'll be out of here and safe in a little bit. Where are your car keys?"

"I don't know. Probably in my purse, but I don't know where my purse is."

"Would you have left them in the Expedition?" I asked.

"Not usually, but today I might have. I was too scared to think straight."

"No big deal. We should be able to call from the house once those guys leave." I wondered, though, if they would leave without first finding Poole.

"How did you find me?" Sylvia asked.

"I saw you driving out of town. I was heading back into town from the Hasbens'. You had mentioned to me that you'd be at your office all day. You had a guy in the Expedition with you, and you didn't look right."

"And based on just that, you followed me?" She looked impressed.

"Well, you did save me once," I said.

She put her arms around me and kissed me. "My hero," she said with a silly grin on her face.

"I think that blow to your head might be affecting your judgment."

"It must be," she said and kissed me again. "Too bad there's all this cactus around."

"Don't forget Poole's accomplices." I figured the blow to her head still had an effect on her. No way I could get amorous right now.

"Do you think he really killed Wally?" she asked.

"Yes. He must have been involved with Lunce. I don't have any idea who these other two are."

"Scary. How long do we have to wait here?"

"Not much longer," I said. That's what I hoped anyway. "Does anyone else live nearby?"

"No. I mean she has neighbors, but I believe the nearest house is at least a mile or two away. I wouldn't even know which way to walk to get to one." She scanned the horizon while she spoke.

I did too, but there was nothing to see. I saw that our rattlesnake hadn't moved. The snake blended in with the ground around it. I was glad Sylvia had seen it and pointed it out to me.

"Look at my hands," she said. "They're still shaking."

I thought mine probably were also. "What's your vote? Should we head away from the house, or should we try to get back to it?"

"What do you mean? Why would we go away from it?" she asked.

"To get further away from these guys."

"Yeah, but then Poole would have a chance to escape. And what would we do out there?"

I liked her thinking. "You're right. I just don't want anything more to happen to you."

That brought a smile to her face. "I vote we give them a few more minutes to look around. They may leave. Then we head back to the house."

"It's a plan. How's your head? Are you going to be okay?" I asked.

"I think so. My head hurts, but I'm no longer dizzy or nauseous. Now I'm only a little scared for both of us. Is my head still bleeding?" She turned her head to the side, and I spread her hair to get a closer look.

"It's stopped, but you do need to get it looked at and cleaned professionally. It may or may not require some stitches, but it needs to be looked at."

I leaned back against the natural rock wall. I watched the hole where we stashed Poole. As long as he didn't climb out or get the makeshift gag off, we stood a chance. Sylvia leaned in close and whispered, "What do you think he does?"

"What do you mean?"

"He works here in the area as kind of a handy man, a jack of all trades, I guess you could say. I know that," she said, "but is that just a cover for what he really does? Is he some mysterious hit man?"

"I think the blow to your head is getting to you. The guy is simply a worthless--"

"No, I know that," she interrupted. "I just said it wrong. Who is he really?"

"Poole?"

"Yes. Why is he doing this? Why was he involved in that girl's death? I thought the guy who was killed, you know, the one they took you to identify that morning, was supposed to be her killer."

"No one knows for sure who killed who right now," I said. "Although the remarks Poole made to you earlier certainly suggest he had something to do with the girl's death."

Sylvia nodded. "And that's what I don't get. Why is he working out here, if he's involved with some criminal organization in Austin?"

"If we get a chance, we or the police can ask him that. I know that crime organizations that run prostitutes use spotters to find them new girls."

"I imagine you don't mean volunteers, either," she said.

"No, I don't. You'd be surprised. They use cabbies, employees at bus stations, a bunch of otherwise non-criminals who, for a few bucks, don't mind pointing out a potential victim to a pimp."

"That's sick."

"Welcome to the world."

"But that still doesn't fit Poole, unless those people also kill people."

"No," I said. "You're right. Poole's role was beyond that. I kind of think that Lunce, the dead guy who kidnapped Frances from coffee shop, did most of the spotting, but I'm not sure of that either."

"Well, hopefully, we'll both live long enough to find out." She wrapped her arms around me and snuggled against me.

I thought back to a time many years ago when I was a young agent with the Air Force Office of Special Investigations. I remembered a surveillance that I was on that went to hell in a split second.

Three of us had set up a surveillance of a fair-sized drug purchase. The buyer was a civilian contractor who had access to the air force base. We believed he was a major supplier of narcotics to base personnel. I had a position in a rundown building across the street from where our source told us the transaction would take place. My two fellow investigators had positions about a quarter mile away in opposite directions, covering the only street to and from the location. They had great spots to photo anyone coming and going down the street. Hypothetically, they could also see the transaction location, but they were too far away and their angles were not good. I had the best seat in the house for the close-in photography. We did not intend to try to arrest anyone. We were simply trying to gather evidence.

Everything started off as planned. However, once all the suspects arrived, they crossed the street and came into my building. Our information had only been partially correct. I found myself hiding in a second floor office behind a large pile of rubble. Fortunately, they must have expected the old building to be empty, because once inside, they only did a cursory inspection. I heard someone come up to the second floor and walk around. After staying for only a few seconds, probably just to glance into each room, he went back downstairs. I was safe as long as I didn't make any noise, or they didn't return to do a more thorough search.

I turned the volume to my hand-held radio to its lowest position. Cell phones were still a luxury at the time. I didn't know if my two fellow agents had seen the group move into the building or not. Grit and debris covered the floor. Walking could give me away, so I remained still. I could hear bits of the conversation from the floor below. The voices I heard sounded angry. I had counted five individuals in all. One man, a person whom I thought I had seen before, accompanied our target. The remaining three arrived in a separate car. Based on our intelligence, these three supplied the drugs to our target.

Those three didn't have the clean cut look of the military contractor we were investigating. The three looked like the stereotypical drug dealers. They also looked dangerous. I was armed, but one against five made miserable odds. I kept my head down and stayed quiet. One of the things that I remembered worrying about was sneezing in that dusty room.

In the end, they left without noticing me, but I failed to get any evidence of a drug transaction. I did have photographs of all of the individuals during their arrival. My team also had some good shots of their vehicles coming and going. From these photos, we determined that our target had met with known, local drug dealers. We also identified our target's associate as another individual who worked on base as a civilian in the motor pool. In the end, the effort hadn't been a total waste. It took another month before we finally busted everyone in a joint effort with the city cops.

For me, however, the bust turned out sort of anticlimactic. The fact that I had survived a very dangerous situation for the first time in my investigative career had made a bigger impression on me. I knew that hiding behind a pile of bricks and trash was nothing to brag about, but in a way it made me feel like I had earned another merit badge.

My mind came back to the present when I heard the sound of someone walking close by. He sounded above us and five or ten yards behind us. I instinctively crouched and held my index finger to my lips. Sylvia reacted with me. The individual continued in a direction that took him away from the path I had followed coming down to the lake. I thought that meant we were safe. The path would have provided a gentle slope down to this level.

The person stopped or moved onto a surface that deadened the sound of breaking twigs and crunching debris. I almost said something to Sylvia about it being safe when a man leaped off the ledge about fifteen yards away. He landed on the hard ground with a grunt. In his left hand he held onto a large revolver.

Sylvia gasped and the man looked at us.

"Hey! What are you doing here?" he snarled.

"Come on, man," I said. "Can't a fellow and his girl get away for a while?" I pulled Sylvia closer to me, which wasn't really necessary as she was already clinging to me.

He looked at us. I knew he had to be trying to make up his mind what to do. He continued pointing the revolver at us. He moved closer to us, paralleling the rock ledge behind us.

"Sugar," I said. "Look at me, darling. I think we should head home. Don't you?" I hadn't planned on my comments to have any real effect on anyone. I simply didn't want Sylvia to warn the jerk with the gun about the big mistake he was about to make.

A lot of people don't know that rattlesnakes have learned over the last hundred or two years that rattling sometimes only gets them killed. This one didn't make a sound until it sunk its fangs deep into the man's right leg. Even then, the snake's rattle wasn't half as loud as the man's screams. Terrified, the poor guy started screaming and jumped around in no particular direction. The snake struck a second time, hitting him just above the left ankle. The man fell to the ground in fear. His feet flailed at the snake but never made contact. The snake decided it was time to leave and slithered away.

Seeing the snake leave brought a little sense back to the man, and he stopped screaming and flailing around. Instead, he started shooting at the snake and calling it about every obscenity in the book. His hands shook with adrenalin or fear. Despite firing repeatedly at the snake, he never hit it. The snake did accelerate his departure and darted behind a distant cactus.

"He's gone, man," I said. "Did he get you?"

"We need to get you to the hospital," Sylvia said, playing along.

"I've been bitten!" the man yelled. "My God, I've been bitten by a rattlesnake!" The man sat up and yanked at the legs of his jeans. He pulled up his jeans and exposed the snake bite on his left leg. The snake had definitely gotten him. "Ooohhh," he moaned.

"Listen, we need to find a phone to call for an ambulance. Do you have one?"

"Yes," the man had started crying. He fumbled with a jeans pocket and held out his phone.

"I'll get someone here real fast. You just try to stay calm," I said. I walked a few yards away. I thought about wrestling the revolver away from him, but decided calling 911 would be a smarter move. "Talk to him," I said to Sylvia.

I heard her ask the guy to show her where the second bite got him while I walked toward the water. Fortunately, the 911 operator answered right away. I explained our predicament and asked for immediate police assistance. As an afterthought, I mentioned the snakebite. I finished the call. When I turned to walk back to the man and Sylvia, the second man appeared on the path above us. He had a pistol in his hand and pointed it my way.

"There's a guy out here who's been bitten by a rattlesnake," I shouted at him. I stayed still not wanting to give him any reason to pull the trigger. "I called for an ambulance."

He looked unsure what to do. After a few seconds he walked close to the edge and looked over at his buddy. "Eddie! Are you okay? What was that shooting I heard?"

"A damn snake! He got me, Robby. I'm hurt."

That worked as I hoped it would. Robby jumped off the ledge and ran over to Eddie.

"Look, man, look! That damn snake bit me. He's over there," Eddie pointed to the cactus where we last saw the rattlesnake. "Go kill him!"

Robby looked for a second like he was going to hunt down the snake, but then he turned his attention toward us.

"Who the hell are you?" he asked. He had a mean looking face.

"Hey, come on. We were just out on a picnic. Our stuff is just over there on the other side of that big oak. We were just walking around the pond when we met Eddie." I didn't want to introduce Sylvia, because for the life of me, I couldn't remember if I had given a false name a few minutes earlier to Eddie. He didn't seem to be paying any attention, but I didn't want to risk it.

"Where's your shirt?" he asked.

"I didn't need it a few minutes ago. Over there," I motioned toward our fictitious picnic spot.

"Good thing I put mine back on," Sylvia said and squeezed my arm. "Why are you guys running around with guns anyway?"

"You best mind your own business," Robby said.

"Robby, I need to get to a doctor. I'm starting to feel sick and my legs hurt like hell."

"Just wait a minute, Eddie. Something doesn't smell right here."

"What are you talking about? Who or what do you think we are?" I asked.

"You see another guy here today?" Robby asked.

"Maybe an hour ago, I saw a couple walking over there." I pointed in a direction that would take them away from the pond. "From the oak by our tree over there, I could see them walking like they were going to check out the grape vines at the very back of the field. I didn't see them come back, but then again we weren't paying much attention to anything after that." I gave a conspiratorial smile to Sylvia.

"They don't need to hear all that," she said.

"You say you have an ambulance coming?" It definitely looked like Robby's mind was trying to decide what to do.

"That's right."

"The police?" Robby asked.

"Not unless they usually respond to snake bites. I guess they could, though," I said.

"Hell, Eddie, why did you get yourself bit?" Robby asked. Eddie moaned again but didn't answer. "Let me have this so you won't have to answer any questions." He took the revolver from Eddie. "I'll go watch for the ambulance."

I figured he was going to drive off before the cops came and leave Eddie to fend for himself. He started jogging toward the end of the path. His departure from the area didn't bother me in the least. He had reached the path and started up the small incline when our good fortune disappeared.

Poole called out for help. His voice sounded muffled, but I didn't think Robby could've missed it. Robby stopped and looked around.

I took Sylvia's hand and pulled on it to get her attention. I didn't want us to be caught looking over at the hole. If Poole stayed quiet, Robby might leave. I looked at Eddie. He had wrapped himself in a fetal position. Soft moans continued to escape from his clenched jaws. The sun suddenly felt awfully hot on my bare back.

"What are we going to do?" Sylvia whispered.

"Somebody help me!" Poole shouted again.

"I'll distract him, and you make a run for your car or the house. Move slowly until the time is right," I said.

"But--"

"No buts, the cops should be here soon," I said.

"Over here," I shouted to Robby and hurried toward the hole that Poole originally intended to be a shallow grave for Sylvia. He had dug it about two feet deep and barely wide or long enough to accommodate a person. Poole just fit into it, and our rush job to cover him did more to dispose of the pile of dirt than cover him. Only a couple inches of dirt hid parts of his body. I now regretted that we didn't cover his face.

"My God! A man's been buried here!" I stepped away and tried to look surprised, knowing all along I was only delaying the inevitable.

Robby approached the hole and saw Poole. With his back now to her, Sylvia started running up the path and away from us.

"Get me out of here!" Poole shouted. He looked more terrified than hurt, although he had a fair sized bruise around his left eye and temple. I knew the back of his head sported an even worse bruise. My shirt wrapped around his neck like a loose-fitting scarf.

"Call 911!" Eddy suddenly screamed at us. He looked like he was trying to stand up. "Please hurry! I'm going to die!"

Robby looked at Eddie but ignored him. Fortunately, he didn't look to see where Sylvia moved to, or he might have seen her as she disappeared into the trees. He turned his attention back to Poole.

"What happened to you?" he asked Poole.

From his hole, Poole looked at me, and I could see his eyes trying to focus. I sensed slow recognition.

The time had come to make my move. I knew any further delay would only allow Poole to say something and make Robby aware of the situation. That would ruin any advantage I had. Robby had already stashed Eddie's revolver in his belt, so I chopped as hard as I could at the wrist of the hand that held the pistol. I had the element of surprise, but I didn't have a good angle. He managed to hang onto the weapon, but the blow did enough to cause him to reach for the pistol with his other hand.

My first thought was to go for the pistol, but he had partially turned away from me. I knew I wouldn't be able to reach the weapon before he had a good grip on it again. I went with Plan B and smashed a left hook into the side of his head. I aimed at the temple, and my fist landed on his ear. His reaction indicated to me that the blow had hurt him. I dove into him and grabbed his gun hand.

The two of us rolled around on the ground for a few seconds. I managed to make him let go of the pistol, and with a quick motion I brushed it away from us. His attention, as did mine, turned to Eddie's revolver in his belt. Neither one of us would have scored any style points while we continued to roll around lashing out at each other.

He snarled a few choice comments at me that mostly ended with words implying he was going to kill me. I didn't say anything. I focused every bit of strength I had on keeping the revolver in his belt. My luck in our hand-to-hand struggle finally came to an end. He broke free and jumped away from me. A good ten feet separated us when he straightened up, drew the revolver, and pointed it at my head.

"You don't need to do this," I said. "Think about what you are about to do. I've already called the police. You don't have a chance of getting away with this. They know about Poole and the girls." I knew I was wasting my breath, but the words seem to force themselves out of my mouth in a continuing stream.

He spit some dirt and blood out of his mouth, but his face was just something in the background. My eyes and mind focused on the large opening of the revolver's barrel aimed at me. His hands weren't steady as they gripped the revolver, and I watched the end of the barrel shake. The movement of the barrel was not enough to make him miss at this distance. We were too close. However, for some silly reason the movement kept my eyes fixated.

He grinned and pulled the trigger.

Chapter 18

Click. Another click. Good old Eddie. It dawned on me that he must have fired every bullet in the revolver at the rattlesnake. It seemed to take a second for both of us to react. His eyes went to his own pistol on the ground about fifteen feet away from him. Unfortunately, I was a lot further away from it.

I didn't have the strength to go another round. He seemed to sense that and smiled.

He went for the pistol, and I sprinted in the opposite direction toward the path. I skipped taking the path, vaulted the four feet to the top of the ledge, and felt the round race by my head the same time I heard the blast from the gun. Only a few feet from the trees and bushes, I instinctively dove to the ground and rolled behind the nearest bush. I went as fast as I could on all fours until I had a few larger bushes and a couple of tree trunks between Robby and me. I glanced back hoping he wouldn't be chasing me. A flash of clothing through the foliage dashed my hopes.

Two things entered my mind as I ran. First, I needed to outrun Robby. Second, I had to lead him away from Sylvia. I ran toward the rear of the large building where they made the wine. Sylvia would have run to the house and her car. A bullet slammed into the wall of the building as I neared it. I zigged to my left. Someone shouted stop or something similar, but I zagged back to my right. Several shots were fired all at once. I reached the edge of the building.

Only then did I realize someone had called me by name.

"West! West! It's okay now."

I recognized the voice. It belonged to Deputy Jerry Stephens. I looked around the corner of the building, breathing heavily and still not too sure what all had just happened. Jerry Stephens and two other deputies slowly approached Robby's body. He didn't look like he'd be a threat to anyone ever again.

"There are two more down by the pond. I don't think they pose much of a threat, but use caution," I rasped. Somewhat breathless, I walked toward Stephens.

One of the deputies I didn't know gave me a look that even I could translate as a sarcastic "Really? Use caution??"

"We will," Jerry said a little more politely. "Stay here."

"One may not be readily visible unless you walk down to the pond. Larry Poole is your killer. He's in a little hole."

Stephens just nodded, and the three of them proceeded to the path.

Two more deputies and a paramedic rounded the corner of the house and jogged toward the other deputies. They looked at me curiously but let me pass by without any questions. When I reached the front of the house, I saw Sylvia sitting on a gurney that looked like it had come out of the ambulance parked in front of the house. A female paramedic was treating the wound on the back of Sylvia's head. A Fredericksburg police sedan and a third sheriff's vehicle sped down the long drive toward the house with lights flashing.

I finally felt a sense of relief. Reinforcements were here in an overwhelming number. By the time I reached Sylvia's side, the two law enforcement vehicles were parking, and I saw a second EMT truck coming down the drive.

"Think she's okay?" I asked the paramedic treating Sylvia's

head wound.

"I wouldn't know. Just met her," she said. "But we'll need to get an X-ray of her skull to determine the extent of the injury."

Sylvia smiled at the paramedic's attempt at humor. I wasn't really in the mood, but she had answered my question.

"How about you?" the paramedic asked.

"I'm okay." I turned to see who had arrived in the Fredericksburg police car.

"Jesus! Jim, what did you do to your back?" Sylvia asked.

"Look at you," the paramedic said. I noticed her name tag said Julie and a last name that had a dozen or so letters in it.

"What about me, Julie?" I asked.

"Looks like you rolled around on a thorn bush."

"A cactus?"

"No, one of those plants with leaves covered with sharp little spines. They're nasty. Stand still for a second, and I'll get those off you."

I remembered when I rolled into the underbrush, after Robby took his first shot at me, that it felt like a few thorns got me. In the excitement - a much better sounding word than terror - of my ongoing attempt to get away, they had only been a nuisance, and I had forgotten about them.

It turned out that Julie didn't treat my back. One of the arriving emergency medical technicians, a tall skinny kid named Joey, carefully pulled the spines out of my back and treated the cuts and scratches. He looked at the growing bruises on my face and concluded that I would survive. He did offer me a couple of Tylenols, but feeling macho at the moment, I declined.

While Joey worked on me, Julie and the other paramedic who had arrived with Joey jumped into the second emergency services vehicle and drove over the lawn toward the pond. I figured someone had called them for help with Eddie.

Sylvia must have been thinking the same thing. "I hope they didn't wait too long to get to him."

"You mean, Eddie, the guy with the snakebite?"

"Yeah."

"They couldn't go until they got the all clear. It's a good sign that everyone's safe. Besides, I'd like to give that rattlesnake a medal."

"Me, too," Sylvia said.

Joey, trying to look busy, dabbed at Sylvia's wound. I could see the curiosity eating away at him.

"What happened out there?" he finally asked.

Sylvia appeared willing to talk to him about it, so I stayed out of the conversation. Another city police vehicle slowly rolled down the driveway toward us. Lieutenant Martin and Officer Cat Morris climbed out of the vehicle when it stopped. They apparently could see something from their angle that I couldn't. Martin waved and smiled at someone, and they both walked across the lawn toward the pond. Cat glanced at me and smiled.

I watched them to see who they had seen, and in a few seconds, Deputy Stephens and a second deputy came into view. The four stopped and talked. I could see Stephens point back toward the pond and then at us. While they talked, another deputy walked by them escorting a handcuffed Larry Poole. He looked dirty and mad, but despite our fight and my striking him with the shovel, he walked like he wasn't hurt at all.

A county crime scene van arrived. I thought about my shirt and wondered if I would ever see it again. A silly thought, I realized. I didn't want it back. It had been in Poole's mouth, and I knew deep down that he had played a major role in Frances Wilikin's murder. He also had every intention of killing Sylvia. The shirt had served a useful purpose as a gag, but I no longer wanted it.

"Jim," Sylvia said.

"Yes."

"How did you get all those scars?"

"There aren't that many," I said. I knew my chest, shoulders, and back had a few scars from either being sliced, stabbed, or shot. "Most I got from being at the wrong place at the wrong time."

"Like today, I suppose."

"I don't think I got any new ones today. Did I?" I asked.

"No, I don't think so. I want to thank you again for following me out here. You saved my life. I don't know how I can ever repay you."

"Leave an open breakfast tab for me at your mom's café. That would be more than enough. Besides, saving beautiful women is what I do," I said. Sylvia smiled at the remark. I meant it as a joke, but it stirred up the vision of Benjamin Lunce dragging Frances Wilikin out of the small coffee shop while I stood there doing nothing. My smile faded from my face.

"You sure you're okay?" Sylvia asked.

"Yes."

"I promise you'll never ever have to pay for a breakfast again at Emma's World Finest Cafe."

"Then we're even," I said.

"Sylvia, I'm so glad you're all right," Deputy Stephens said. He grabbed both of Sylvia's hands with his.

I figured he wanted to hug her but didn't think this was the proper place or time. I could see genuine concern in his eyes.

"Just a nasty bump on the head, but it doesn't even hurt anymore," she said.

"The medics said I could run you to the clinic in Fredericksburg. That is if you don't mind riding with me. I need to go that way anyway. Can I give you a lift?" he asked.

"Of course," she said. "What about Jim?"

Jerry looked at me. "Sylvia told me when I arrived that you rescued her. I want to thank you for that. You're welcome to come with us."

"No thanks. My car is here, and I don't need to go to the hospital." I believed he meant the thank you, but doubted that he really wanted me to join them on the ride into town.

As the two walked off, I noticed that Sylvia hung onto his arm. I glanced over at Joey, the young guy who had taken the thorny leaves out of my back. He had probably been listening to my conversations and wondered what was going on. I saw Officer Cat Morris walking toward me. I went to meet her.

She shook her head and grinned. "I don't even want to know why you're half undressed and out here with Sylvia Scott."

"I wish that was it, Cat. It's not been a pleasant afternoon."

"I saw your gal leave with Stephens. They looked pretty chummy. You okay with that?" she asked.

"Yes, I really am. She's never been my girl, Cat. You know, though, I'd love to take you back to that restaurant you took me to, eat more ribs, and drink a lot more beer."

"I have a thing about dating men who have just been jilted. Sorry. However, if you find a shirt to put on, I'll be happy to drive you to the station and take your statement."

"I wasn't jilted," I said. "Isn't this in the county's jurisdiction?"

"Yes, but this is a joint case. They're going to handle the scene including the dead body, the two prisoners, and I think Deputy Stephen's going to personally see to Ms. Scott." She couldn't resist trying to rib me. "The Lieutenant and I get you. He said he'd prefer to stay and watch the effort here. I couldn't reach Officer Creighton, so I'm stuck with you."

"I have another shirt in the car," I said. "I thought you were going south to do that interview."

"That fell apart as quickly as it got arranged. They called and said Loretta wasn't where they thought she would be. Said they'd call us once they found her."

"Too bad, but I imagine they'll find her soon," I said. We walked to my Mustang, and I grabbed a shirt.

"Ever put the roof down?" she asked.

"All the time."

"Cool, let's go back in style," she said.

We didn't talk on the drive into town. She turned the car's radio to a local station she liked, leaned back, closed her eyes, and enjoyed the ride. I saw a phone store that advertised my carrier at a strip mall shortly after we entered the city limits. When I turned into the parking lot, Cat came back to life.

"What are you doing?" she asked.

I explained to her my predicament with my phone. "I need maybe five minutes to see if they can salvage my data and transfer it into a new phone."

I'm not sure how I expected Cat to respond, but she took the delay in stride. She wondered around the small store looking at all the different phones on display, and a short, chubby employee with greasy, spiked hair worked his magic for me. In ten minutes, I had a new functioning cell phone with the same number and all my old data, and we were on our way again.

At the police station, Cat walked me through the interview starting from when I saw Sylvia drive by me on Highway 290. She stopped the recording at the point where Stephens or his partner shot the man I only knew as Robby. She followed up with questions that once again impressed me with her attention to detail.

Toward the end of the interview my new phone started buzzing like crazy. I ignored it. Someone peeked into the room and told us that the incident was on the evening news. I figured correctly that the news had been the catalyst for the phone calls and texts. After the interview ended, Cat asked me to sit tight for a few minutes.

"Okay, that's it," she said when she returned. "You're free to go."

"Sure I can't buy you dinner first?" I asked.

In typical Cat fashion, she ignored my question.

"The guy who was bitten by the rattlesnake talked up a storm today. He claimed that Poole killed both Wilikin and Montrose. He and his partner were out at the winery only to give Poole a ride. They knew he was getting rid of another witness, a woman, but that was all. He claimed neither Robby nor he knew who she was."

"Poole talking?"

"Nope, but he's toast," she said.

"How about Lunce? Any more on his involvement?"

"According to the guy with the snake bite, he let the girl, Frances, get away. Apparently, before she escaped, she saw some things she shouldn't have."

"Did he say what?" I asked.

"Not specifically, at least not yet, but Lunce had orders to bring her back. I guess his butt was on the line for letting her get away."

"It's a good break that Eddie is talking."

"He seems to want to throw all the blame on Poole. He doesn't know that his partner is dead, or he might conveniently blame him for everything. Supposedly, Poole has a lot of money. Poole hangs out here in the Hill Country in an attempt to develop an identity as a hard working country boy who visits Austin on occasion. In reality, Eddie claims that Poole is fairly high up in a criminal organization based in Austin. Eddie doesn't seem to like him. Says he's a spoiled rich kid."

"How about that? Should make Austin PD happy," I said.

"Very much so."

"Not hungry?" I asked again, knowing that as usual she had purposely ignored my earlier question.

"Go home. You're cleared to leave the city, the county, the state. We know how to reach you if we need you. It's late, but you should still be able to get there around midnight your time."

"You're a good cop, Ms. Cat. I hope you stay with it."

She walked me out to the car. "I doubt if this goes to a full trial. Eddie has already given us more than enough to work with. Poole will likely get a fancy lawyer and plead out. It would be in his best interest. I bet it's his DNA we found in the

Wilikin murder."

I nodded in agreement.

"If it goes to trial, or if you ever get back this way just to visit, we'll do that dinner again." She held out her hand, and I shook it.

"It's a deal," I said.

"Now go on," she said. She smiled and waved as I drove off.

I could see lighting off in the distance, but it looked like the storm had passed us by.

Chapter 19

I didn't drive straight out of town. For the last time, I stopped at the local coffee shop. While I did purchase a cup of coffee for the road, the stop had more to do with closure than the caffeine. The only employee whom I recognized there was the older barista, the one who had tried to stop Cisco's bleeding from the gunshot wound. She surprised me by recognizing me.

"You're still here," she said.

"Leaving tonight," I said and resisted an urge to ask her why she said what she had. After all, this was a small town.

"That was you at the shooting today with Sylvia, wasn't it?"

"Yes."

"I'm glad you're okay. I understand Sylvia is going to be fine, too."

"You're a step ahead of me," I said.

"In addition to my job here, I work part time at her mother's café," she said.

Everything fell in place. "How's Cisco doing?"

"He's going to make a full recovery. He's a good guy. We all hope he'll return here to work when he's able."

"Good."

"The whole thing was such a shame," she said.

"Yes, it was. How are you handling all this?" I asked her.

"Me? I guess okay."

"I heard some of the baristas quit."

"Can you blame them?" she asked.

"No, not really. I'm glad you're still around."

"Thanks. A long time ago, I had a husband who used to knock me around. I finally made up my mind not to let bullies intimidate me anymore. Don't get me wrong. They still frighten me. That guy, you know the guy who came in here with the gun, he really scared me. I just won't let them dictate how I live or what I do anymore."

"Good for you."

I glanced at my new phone before I drove out of town. I counted eight missed messages or calls. I decided not to answer any of them, but then changed my mind. I returned a text message from Sylvia. She said she wanted to thank me again and that her mother had wholeheartedly agreed with the free breakfasts. In my return text, I simply said thanks and that getting to know her was the one rose in an otherwise weedy visit to Fredericksburg. I reread my text before sending it and knew right away that I'd never make it as a romantic poet. I sent it anyway.

I drove out of town and headed toward Mason, Eden, and beyond. The day's events swirled through my mind. I thought about the rattlesnake that bit Eddie. During my interview, Cat made one remark that had stuck with me. After I told her about Robby trying to shoot me with Eddie's empty revolver, Cat had said, "Got to love those rattlesnakes." Even the thought of it brought a smile to my face. I hoped that Lieutenant Martin and the Chief realized what a talented professional they had in Cat Morris.

After I passed the eighth deer grazing next to the highway in the late evening darkness, I decided to call it a night and found a place to stay in Big Spring, Texas. I only had another three to four hours of driving, but I had no desire to hit a deer while on my way home. Besides, the deer felt like an omen telling me to cool it, that I had pressed my luck far enough for one day. I grabbed a hamburger and ate it in my room. More importantly, I took an overdue shower, getting the last of the pond scum off me.

The reflection of my face in the mirror didn't worry me. I'd have a few bumps and bruises for a couple days, but otherwise I felt and looked fine.

I took my phone out and decided to return a number of the texts and calls made to me earlier in the day. I was surprised to learn how many people whom I had met only briefly in Fredericksburg had reached out to say that they were happy I was okay. Most I could respond to with a short thank-you text. The only one I deleted without responding to was from Lynn, Fredericksburg's overly-friendly realtor. Her comments were harmless, but I noticed she had included a link to a website. Despite the temptation, I didn't click on the link. It may have only been to her business webpage, but I didn't need to find out. I had enough clutter in my brain for one trip already.

Despite the late hour, I called Tom and Brenda rather than send them a text. They wanted all the details. After five minutes I was able to plead a headache and told them I would give them another call in a few days after everything had settled down.

My response to Glo I held off to last. I didn't know what more I could really say to her, and she hadn't asked for anything. Her brief text said that she and Bell were very happy that Frances' murderers were going to have to face justice. They were also pleased that I was unharmed in the process. She finished her short text by saying, "Thank you for being there."

I didn't know what to say to her. It pleased me, too, the way things had turned out, but I didn't feel like a hero. She kept me in the investigation, just like Tom and his friends had earlier by telling me stuff they expected me to tell the police. For the most part, I still felt like everyone's pawn. I finally wrote a short text telling her that I was also happy that the whole thing appeared to be over. I wished her the very best and asked her to relay my thanks to Bell. It was an inadequate message, but I didn't know what else to say. Maybe in a few days I could come up with some wiser and wittier comments to send to her.

For my part, I knew I had gotten a few lucky breaks. I couldn't explain it, but I didn't lie in bed and think of Eddie's revolver pointed at my head. Maybe that would bother me later, but maybe not. The last thing I thought of before I fell asleep that night was Cat's remark. "Gotta love those rattlesnakes."

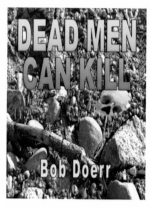

Title: *Dead Men Can Kill*™
Author: Bob Doerr
Publisher: TotalRecall Publications, Inc.
Format: HARDCOVER, 6.14" x 9.21"
Number of pages: 320
13-digit ISBN: 978-1-59095-758-5
Publication: December 8, 2009

When Jim West, a former Air Force Special Agent with the Office of Special Investigations, moves back to New Mexico, his goal is simple: start an easy going second career as a professional lecturer on investigative techniques to colleges and civic organizations. He never envisioned that his practical demonstration of forensic hypnosis on stage with a state university student would stir up memories of an 18-year old murder mystery. When the student is murdered three days later, West finds himself ensnared in a web of intrigue that pits him and the small town's authorities against a ruthless, psychotic killer.

An aggressive reporter for the town newspaper seeks out West for help with the story, but after one of her co-workers is murdered, she quickly aligns her efforts with West and the Sheriff. As West works closely with her, he begins to wonder if this could be the first real relationship for him since his devastating divorce a few years earlier.

The killer, though, has other plans for the reporter and the story takes fascinating twists and turns, leading to an inevitable, riveting confrontation.

Look out for a new hero on the mystery/thriller landscape! Jim West, retired military investigator, is resourceful, intuitive, pragmatic and always competent. All of West's abilities are tested when he matches wits with psychopathic serial killer William White, a man whose appreciation for murder is surpassed only by his delight in domination. Bob Doerr has crafted a must-read addition to the genre in Dead Men Can Kill, which evolves from absorbing story to absolute page-turner as West closes in on a killer who is supposedly dead. Highly recommended!

--Dallin Malmgren, author of...

The Whole Nine Yards   The Ninth Issue   Is This for a Grade?

A Jim West™ Mystery/Thriller

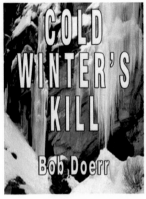

Title: *Cold Winter's Kill*™
Author: Bob Doerr
Publisher: TotalRecall Publications, Inc.
Format: HARDCOVER, 6.14" x 9.21"
Number of pages: 288
13-digit ISBN: 978-1-59095-762-8
Publication: Dec 8, 2009

Cold Winter's Kill is a fast paced thriller that takes place in the scenic mountains of Lincoln County, New Mexico and throws Jim West into a race against time to stop a psychopath who abducts and kills a young blonde every Christmas...

It was one of those phone calls former Air Force Special Agent Jim West never wanted to receive--an old friend calling to ask if he could drive down to Ruidoso, New Mexico to help locate his daughter who has disappeared while on a ski trip with friends. Jim found himself heading to Ruidoso even though he believed, much like the local authorities, that if she had gone missing in the mountains in December, her survival chances were slim. He didn't want to be there when they found her, but still he drove on.

Once in Ruidoso, Jim discovers a sinister coincidence that changes everything. It appears that someone is abducting and killing one young blond every year around Christmas. The race is on--can Jim locate his friend's daughter in time? But why is this happening and who's doing it?

Jim can't wait for the local authorities to raise the priority of their search, or for the pending blizzard to pass. In his haste he puts himself in the killer's sights. Will he, too, suffer from a cold winter's kill?

"GREAT SUSPENSE! In *Cold Winter's Kill* Bob Doerr grabs your attention from the beginning and holds it until the last sentence. Hard to put down!"
>   --*Shelba Nicholson*
>   former Women's Editor, *Texarkana Gazette*

A Jim West™ Mystery/Thriller

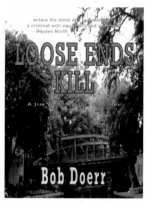

Title: *Loose Ends Kill*™
Author: Bob Doerr
Publisher: TotalRecall Publications, Inc.
Format: HARDCOVER, 6.14″ x 9.21″
Number of pages: 288
13-digit ISBN: 978-1-59095-717-2
Publication: Oct 27, 2010

LOOSE ENDS KILL is a fast paced mystery/thriller that takes place in the historic city of San Antonio, Texas, and throws Jim West into the middle of a police investigation of the murder of an old friend's wife. The police already believe they have the killer in custody – West's friend.

West is drawn into this mystery by a call from the old friend who requests his assistance. West agrees to help his friend and digs deep to try to find another suspect. In the process he soon discovers that he is being followed and targeted for harassment, but by whom?

West quickly discovers that he didn't know his old friend's wife as well as he thought. To his surprise, he learns that she has had a number of affairs dating back for more than a decade. In fact, while investigating the murder, he realizes that his friend and he may be the only two people unaware of her philandering behavior.

Theorizing that one of her lovers could have had just as much motive as her husband, West starts turning over the rocks identifying one lover after another. In doing so, West unintentionally ignites an outbreak of more death and mayhem. The police and his friend's lawyers want West to go back home. The police even threaten to arrest him.

Soon, West believes the real killer wants him gone or dead. Deciding the only way to resolve the case before the outside pressures force him to leave, he sets a trap for the killer using himself as bait. However, he soon learns he may have only outsmarted himself.

A Jim West™ Mystery/Thriller

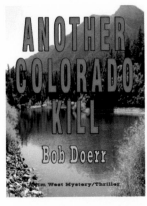

Title: *Another Colorado Kill*™
Author: Bob Doerr
Publisher: TotalRecall Publications, Inc.
Format: HARDCOVER, 6.14" x 9.21"
Number of pages in the finished book: 288
13-digit ISBN: 978-1-59095-784-4
Publication Date: September 06, 2011

It was supposed to be a short, fun golf outing, but when Jim West and his friend Edward "Perry" Mason stumble across a dead body in a restroom at a rest stop along I-25, things turn bad and then only get worse.

With the golf outing shot, West intends to stay in Colorado Springs only for a day or two. However, when two more murder victims turn up – one with West's name handwritten in her notebook - the heat on West skyrockets. The police instruct him to stick around, and soon he discovers that while the police may want to pin the crimes on him, the killer wants him out of the picture. Way out – like dead.

West's only ally is Lieutenant Michelle Prado, a tall red head with large green eyes that captivate West. Assigned to keep an eye on West, Lieutenant Prado decides the best way to do so is to keep him close. West and Prado do their own digging into the investigation. In the process, Jim wonders how close their relationship will evolve.

It seems to West that as the police focus less on him, the killer intensifies his focus on him. Barely surviving an initial confrontation, West realizes he must take the initiative. If he doesn't, or perhaps even if he does - he may end up as just another Colorado kill.

A Jim West™ Mystery/Thriller

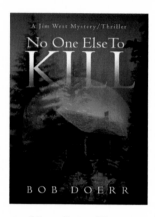

Title: *No One Else To Kill*
Author: Bob Doerr
Publisher: TotalRecall Publications, Inc.
Format: HARDCOVER, 6.14" x 9.21"
13-digit ISBN: 978-1-59095-422-5
  Paper Back: ISBN: 978-1-59095-423-2
  eBook: ISBN: 978-1-59095-424-9
Number of pages in the finished book: 352
Publication Date: December 4, 2012

No One Else to Kill, **Bob Doerr, TotalRecall Publications** - In this newest book in the popular Jim West series, Mr. West finds himself stood up and out of town. Looking forward to some R & R he keeps his reservation at the remote hunting lodge. Located in the Pecos Wilderness area in New Mexico it's a hunter's haven. Expecting to do nothing other than relax, he has no idea what the rest of the weekend holds for him. When a murder takes place, the hotel guest are detained and no one is beyond suspicion. The sheriff is called in, and while the investigation is underway, a second murder takes place. Both crimes are

2013
Eric Hoffer Award
WINNER
Excellence in
Independent
Publishing

clearly related, but by whom and why? With time running out and unable to find a motive, the legal experts seek Jim's help.

2013
da Vinci Eye
FINALIST
Eric Hoffer Award
Excellence in
Independent Publishing

The cover for *No One Else To Kill* is a 2013 finalist for the da Vinci Eye award.
  Bob's four previous novels in the series are titled *Dead Men Can Kill, Cold Winter's Kill, Loose Ends Kill,* and *Another Colorado Kill.* The latter two were selected as Eric Hoffer Award finalists for 2010 and 2011, respectively.

  Bob Doerr's *No One Else To Kill* was awarded the Grand Prize in the "Books With Out Publishers" writing contest at www.ultimateherocontest.com

A Jim West™ Mystery/Thriller

Title: The Enchanted Coin
Author: Bob Doerr
Publisher: TotalRecall Publications, Inc.
Format: HARDCOVER, 6.14" x 9.21"
13-digit ISBN: 978-1-59095-083-8
  Paper Back: ISBN: 978-1-59095-084-5
  Book: ISBN: 978-1-59095-085-2
Number of pages in the finished book: 130
Publication Date: September 17, 2013

We have all heard of tales of UFO's, ghosts, people who say they can talk to the spirits, ancient curses, and magical talismans. Most of us automatically dismiss them as false, figments of people's imagination, and understandably so. However, might not just a few of them be true? I don't know, but I heard this story from a young man the other day who swore the fascinating tale I have set forth in this book really did really occur, because it happened to him. You be the judge.

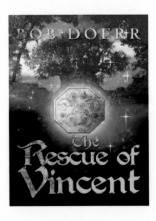

Title: The Enchanted Coin
Author: Bob Doerr
Publisher: TotalRecall Publications, Inc.
Format: HARDCOVER, 6" x 9"
13-digit ISBN: 978-1-59095-083-8
  Paper Back: ISBN: 978-1-59095-084-5
  Book: ISBN: 978-1-59095-085-2
Number of pages in the finished book: 130
Publication Date: September 17, 2013

We have all heard of tales of UFO's, ghosts, people who say they can talk to the spirits, ancient curses, and magical talismans. Most of us automatically dismiss them as false, figments of people's imagination, and understandably so. However, might not just a few of them be true? I don't know, but I heard this story from a young man the other day who swore the fascinating tale I have set forth in this book really did really occur, because it happened to him. You be the judge.

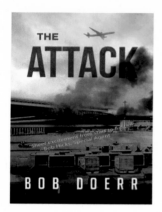

Title: The Attack
Author: Bob Doerr
Publisher: TotalRecall Publications, Inc.
Format: HARDCOVER, 6″ x 9″
13-digit ISBN: 978-1-59095-145-3
  Paper Back: ISBN: 978-1-59095-146-0
  Book: ISBN: 978-1-59095-147-7
Number of pages in the finished book:
Publication Date:

A terrorist team has just set off four explosive devices in an international airport close to New York City. The leader of the terrorists, Ahmad Khalin, survives the attack and plans to attack a second U.S. airport within the month. As Khalin makes his escape from the New York area he is involved in a shooting in Connecticut. Clint Smith, a U.S. government agent assigned to an ultra-secret agency, is at a restaurant across the street when the shooting occurs. He responds to the scene to see if he can help, but Khalin is gone. On a hunch, Teresa Deer, Smith's boss, sends Smith after Khalin. Smith's pursuit takes him to Bar Harbor, Maine; Wiesbaden, Germany; the Costa Brava, Spain; Northern Scotland; Lake of the Woods, Ontario, Canada; and finally into Saskatchewan, Canada, where the final confrontation takes place. Throughout the pursuit, a number of interesting characters add to the subplots and try to survive their involvement in the chase.

Author Bob Doerr Uses his special knowledge to provide authentic details in his novels about how law enforcement agencies do their work.

www.bobdoerr.com